THE DEMON IN THE TAPROOM

A Monstrous New York Novel

E.M. SAUBER

Editing & Proofreading - Nice Girl, Naughty Edits

Cover Design – Impyeu

This one is for anyone who's ever felt they had to change themselves to fit in. Don't dim your light for anyone. Shine bright, my friend, because you matter.

NOTE FROM THE AUTHOR

Dearest reader,

Welcome to Monstrous New York! This series is set in an alternate version of New York City, where monsters and humans live together in harmony… usually. I have taken creative liberties with some of the setting, as well as Penelope' s and Syn's occupations. So use your imagination and allow me to bend reality within the confines of these pages.

This is a sweet sapphic monster romance, but that doesn't mean we can forgo some warnings. If any of the following make you uncomfortable, please consider choosing a different book or proceed with caution.

- Misogynistic comments from side characters
- Verbal/emotional abuse from a parent
- Not being accepted by a parent after coming out
- Chronic illness, including chronic migraines and anxiety
- Maternal death during childbirth (off page)
- Death of a parent (off page)
- Detailed depictions of sex between consenting adults
- Use of profane language
- Potential Spoiler: Yes, this is a cozy, low-stakes romance and Penelope and Syn get their HEA, but Penelope's mom is an awful person, and let's just say, karma is a bitch.

Contents

Chapter 1

Penelope

"What was she thinking?" I murmur, tugging at the hem of the too-short garment. This is awful. "If I bend over and there's someone behind me, they're going to get more than they bargained for." To prove my point, I bend at the waist and glance over my shoulder at the mirror. Sure enough, my tan, panty-covered butt cheeks are on full display.

The shrill ringtone of my phone has me popping to a stand and snatching it off the dresser. As soon as I swipe to accept the call, my mom's perky voice fills my ear. "What do you think of the dress? Isn't it darling?"

"It's... *something*," I drone, hooking a finger into the neckline and pulling it from my flushed skin. The poofy sleeves itch to high heavens, and the sensitive skin on my upper arms is already bright red and splotchy.

"I saw it in the window at this little boutique and just had to get it for you. The color really brings out your eyes."

When I arrived home from work today, there was a delivery waiting for me, courtesy of my mom.

Cerulean irises scan up and down my reflection, and I scowl. "Thank you, Mom." They're the same color as hers.

I'm practically her clone. Same naturally golden-blonde hair. Same short stature and petite frame.

If it were up to her, I'd follow in her footsteps, too. A socialite who married young and hasn't worked a day in her life.

"Now, you're to meet Matthew at the Taproom at seven o'clock sharp. Don't be late, Penelope. It's unbecoming, and I don't want to hear from his mother tomorrow at the club that my daughter lacks punctuality. I raised you better." The reprimand in her tone should sting, but I'm numb to it after almost thirty years of her belittling words.

Rolling my eyes, I unzip the dress. A sigh rattles my chest as I shimmy it off and kick it to the corner of my bedroom, where it will hopefully be swallowed by a black hole. *So much better.*

A navy t-shirt dress hanging in the closet snags my attention. I pull it from the hanger and slip it over my head. The soft, worn cotton wraps around my body like a fluffy cloud, the hem hitting just above my knees. Its high neckline will keep my date from leering all night.

"Are you listening, Penelope?" Her voice rises to a shrill octave, and I fight the urge to hang up on her. As much as I want to ignore her, it never ends well for me.

"*Yes, Mother*. Seven o'clock at The Taproom. I'll be there with bells on."

"There's no need for an attitude, Penelope. Remember, Matthew was recently promoted to senior associate at the firm he works for. He has a bright future ahead of him. If you hit it off, just imagine..." There's an unmistakable hint of joy in her tone as she no doubt pictures the future she has mapped out for me, white picket fence included. "He'll be able to provide for you, and you can finally quit that dreadful job in the city."

Yet again, my job—one of the many points of contention between my mom and I—rears its ugly head. If she had her way, I'd be married with two point five kids and a glamorous house in the Hamptons.

Just like she was at my age.

"I like my job, Mom. I like Annie and Cyrus." *I like my independence and not having to rely on anyone else.*

"Ugh, that *dreadful* dragon woman. I can't even imagine..."

Well, it's a good thing you don't work for her, then. But I keep that thought to myself.

Juggling the phone from hand to hand, I slip on some knee-high boots and a long knit cardigan, just in case the restaurant has the air conditioner blasting. I don't want to freeze to death on top of what's sure to be a horrific date. Cozy and chic—perfect.

"Anyway, be sure to ask him about his job and his hobbies. He's golfing with your father this weekend."

Of course he is. Everyone in my mom's world is connected. What's the point of knowing someone unless they can do something for you?

To her, everyone's a steppingstone to something bigger and better, and if you don't fall in line, you're kicked to the side.

"You know, Penelope, I already had you and Colin by the time I was your age."

"I know, *Mother.*" My eyes roll so far into the back of my head, I'm surprised they don't get stuck there. I'm twenty-eight, but she acts like I'm knocking on death's door.

There's no point arguing with her. Not when it's ingrained into the very threads of her DNA that a woman's sole purpose is to be the picture-perfect wife and mother.

Not that she was a good mother, by any means. Without Dad and Colin, I wouldn't have survived her constant critiques and borderline verbal abuse.

Truth be told, I don't even know if I want kids. Sure, I love my niece and nephew, but I get to send them back to my brother when I get overstimulated.

Honestly, props to Colin and his wife because those kids have limitless energy. I wouldn't be able to handle them 24/7.

"I've got to go, Mom," I say, ready to get this entire evening over with so I can snuggle into bed with a pint of ice cream and my latest book.

"Don't disappoint me... and make sure you smile." Her parting words do nothing to soothe the dread coiled low in my belly about this whole situation.

The gusted breath that leaves my lips ruffles the fly-away hairs that have slipped from my ponytail. Setting my phone on the dresser, I turn to the mirror once again. Frazzled. That's the only word I can use to describe the state of my hair.

Pale-yellow strands of frizz frame my face, and my normally perky ponytail droops from the back of my head.

I wince as I rip out the elastic, grab my brush, and smooth every strand back into place before securing it again. The sleek ponytail is a heavy weight and a constant reminder of yet another similarity between me and Mom.

If she wouldn't blow an absolute gasket, I would shave my head right now. When it's down, my hair trails to the middle of my back.

It's hot.

It's heavy.

It's itchy.

Women have long hair. A fact that was forced into *my* DNA every day of my childhood. As much as I despise the long tresses, they've become a sort of sick and twisted security blanket. But that's an issue for a different day.

My phone pings from its perch on the dresser, reminding me I need to leave now if I want to make it to the Taproom on time.

Hair in place, a modest dress that won't give Matthew any ideas, and comfortable footwear. I'm as ready as I'll ever be.

The dull thrum of my heartbeat fills my ears when I wrap a clammy hand around the S-shaped handle to the restaurant. I've never been here before. New and unfamiliar environments aren't really my thing.

I prefer to stick to my routine. Work and home are my safe zones, with an occasional trip to Cream Me Up, the local monster-owned diner. Although, that usually only happens when I'm accompanied by the few friends I have.

Vibrant laughter and the buzz of murmured conversation surround me as I enter the Taproom. For a Thursday night, it sure is bustling with lively energy. Monsters and humans of all varieties and walks of life fill the tables and booths. Some dressed in casual clothes, others fresh from corporate jobs in suits and ties.

Why would Matthew pick this place for our date? If he's in my mom's circle, I get the impression he's not fond of monsters.

The hostess smiles before asking, "How many?"

I smooth my hands down the front of my dress. "Oh, I'm actually meeting someone. Matthew Cartwright."

"Of course. Right this way," she says, leading me deeper into the crowded space. Everything is sleek and polished. Dark wood tables and booths accented by deep burgundy cushions. Industrial-style Edison bulb fixtures hang from the ceiling, casting everything in a warm glow.

It's what I imagine a speakeasy would look like if they were still around. Intimate and cozy with the right company, something I don't have the luxury of tonight.

As I approach the suit-clad man at the table, I plaster on my biggest, brightest smile, even as a wave of bone-deep exhaustion threatens to take me under. Fake it till you make it, right?

One glance at this man reaffirms what I already knew—this date is going to end badly.

Dark hair slicked to perfection, his face is clean shaven, revealing high cheekbones and full lips. Objectively speaking, Matthew is an attractive man, but he does nothing for me.

No racing heartbeat. No tummy flutters. And certainly no flutters farther south.

"Penelope!" he greets me as he stands. His eyes swing to his watch, and he says, "I was afraid you weren't going to make it."

Both hands on the clock on the mirrored wall behind the bar click to the seven as he pulls me in for a hug. "I thought we agreed on seven?" My brow wrinkles when he tugs me into his body, and an overwhelming wave of cologne clogs my nostrils. I stifle a cough and drape an arm around him in a half-hearted response, but his hand roams lower.

Cupping my bottom, his fingers curl, and he gives a little squeeze.

I stiffen before pressing my hands to his chest and pushing him away. "Sorry." I cough, cheeks burning. "I'm not really a hugger."

His answering smug chuckle has my hackles rising. "I think you'll find I'm *very* affectionate." The wink that follows his creepy statement has my skin crawling and a big, red warning sign flashing in my brain.

I glance over my shoulder at the entrance. If I leave now, maybe Mom won't find out until tomorrow morning.

You know she'll find out sooner. She always does.

Barely managing to stifle my groan, I settle into my chair, and my eyes scan the crowded bar. A large wolven male stands by the emergency exit, with his furry, muscular arms crossed over his broad chest. Surely, he'd come to my rescue if Matthew turns out to be a misogynistic creep.

Based on our first interaction, the chances of that being the case are pretty high.

The wolven gives me a nod, easing my nerves the slightest bit, before I continue assessing my surroundings. Depthless midnight pools have the breath stalling in my lungs. Behind the bar stands the most beautiful creature I've ever laid eyes on.

Messy purple waves fall to her chin, drawing my eyes to her pursed lips. Her dark gaze flits to Matthew, then back to me, the furrow between her sculpted eyebrows deepening.

"And for you, miss?" The waiter's question pulls my attention back to my date.

Before I can pick up the menu, Matthew butts in with, "The lady will have the house salad. Grilled chicken. Dressing on the side—"

My tongue finally decides to work, and I interrupt him. "Actually, could I get a bacon cheeseburger and sweet potato fries?" Slicing my gaze to Matthew's, I paste on a saccharine smile. "I hear they have the best burgers in the city."

The muscles in his jaw jump as he clenches his teeth, and the corners of his lips tic down.

Seems he's just as controlling as Mom. No wonder she thought he'd be the perfect date. *No, thank you.*

Awkward, *uncomfortable* silence thickens the air to a suffocating degree when the waiter leaves with our orders. If I don't at least try to appease Mom, she'll set me up on another date. Swallowing my discomfort, once again, I plaster on my sunny smile. It's become such a comfortable mask over the years that I don't even realize I'm hiding my true feelings from the world most of the time. "So my mom said you were just promoted at work." I don't recognize the perkiness in my voice.

Is this who I've become? Perky Penelope. Always sunny. Always happy. Never one to make waves.

The dark cloud dissipates from Matthew's features, and he smiles. His chest puffs out, stretching the fabric of his pristine white dress shirt. "Yes. The law partners finally realized what they were missing and promoted me to senior associate."

"That's nice."

"It is." The ice cubes in his glass clink as he takes a sip of the amber liquid. "You should consider yourself lucky, Penelope."

My brow collapses. "Oh?"

Matthew nods. "I'll be bringing home a lot more money now, so if *this* goes well"—he waves a hand from me to him—"you could quit your little job."

I think I just threw up in my mouth. Grabbing the glass of water from the table, it washes down the pungent bile as I swallow.

Before I can respond to the blatant insult, Matthew opens his big mouth again. "You should know that I'm a traditional man. A woman's place is in the home, raising the children, and *serving* her husband."

I don't think my jaw can drop any farther than it already has. I'm utterly dumbfounded by my date's blatantly sexist remark. So much so, I can't even form a proper rebuttal.

"Don't you agree?" Matthew's lips twist into a toothy grin that's downright lascivious.

In the next instant, cold liquid soaks the sleeve of my sweater… and Matthew's smug face. White fabric clings to his broad chest, scattering ice cubes as it heaves up and down. "Oops," I quip, biting my lip to hold in my smile when I set the empty glass back on the table.

I'm not sure what came over me. Under normal circumstances, I avoid confrontation like the plague, but his words triggered an uncontrollable urge within me.

It's exhilarating, and my heart slams against the walls of my chest.

"You fucking bitch!" His chair clatters to the floor as he shoots to his feet, face red and eyes burning with rage. The poor, melting ice chunks fall to the ground, too. "What the fuck is wrong with you?"

There's a commotion to my left and a blur of shadows, then a leather-clad figure stands between me and my furious date. Booted feet planted wide and tattooed hands fisted at her sides, she's a menacing presence that I wouldn't want to meet in a dark alley.

Or would I?

Tendrils of black surround her. Purple hair swirls around her head, accentuating the two sets of curved gray horns. Behind her back, her spade-tipped tail cracks against the table like a whip. "I think you need to leave." Her voice is eerily calm considering the commotion surrounding us, but there's a sultry rasp to it that has my stomach somersaulting and my thighs clenching to stave off the dull ache between them.

My dark savior.

The mysterious woman tips her chin to the wolven approaching my soaked and fuming date from behind. "Get this fucker out of here," she seethes, jaw muscle tensing as she turns her head to the side, like the mere sight of Matthew makes her want to hurl.

Same, girl, same.

In the next blink, those midnight eyes are on me, soft and sincere. Her shadows wrap around me like a warm blanket, and I release the breath I was holding. She extends a hand to me. "Are you okay, sweetness?"

Chapter 2

Synthea

Her fingers slide against mine, and I almost combust on the spot. Electricity zips up my arm as I bathe in the delicate touch. My fingers curl around her wrist, and I guide her to stand in front of me.

Overzealous as they may be, my shadows tighten around her, forcing her to step forward until our chests brush. Another burst of that same electric energy. Curious.

Who is this alluring woman?

The sleeve of her sweater grazes my bare bicep when she brings her hands to my chest, the icy bite of the soaked fabric forcing a shiver down my spine, and my shadowy tendrils retract.

A gasp falls from her pouty lips. The woman takes a step back, arms dropping to her sides. Her gaze lowers to the floor as a visible tremble shakes her petite frame. "I-I'm okay. Thank you."

My ears twitch at her hushed words.

I noticed her the second she walked into my bar. This soft creature who wrapped her long cardigan around her body as her shoulders rounded. Tension radiated from her when she sat down across from that asshole. I don't know what he said to make her throw her drink on him, but I'm about to find out.

"Let's get you some water, sweetness." The pet name slips out for the second time in under five minutes. What's this beauty doing to me? One flutter of her long, mascara-coated lashes, one glance at her big blue eyes, and I'm putty in her hands.

When I turn toward the bar, nearly every eye in the place is on me and the woman.

A shrill whistle fills the silence of the bar when I place my fingers to my lips and blow. "Show's over, folks!" I wave a hand in a "carry on" gesture before focusing back on my mysterious companion.

Raucous conversation and laughter fill the air again as I lead the woman toward the bar. Choosing a stool at the end, she takes a seat while I slip behind the lacquered bar top.

One shadowy tendril wraps around a clean glass while another pours a scoop of ice into it before filling it with water. I slide it across the bar to my new infatuation. "I'm Synthea, by the way." With a wink at her, my lips curve into a sultry smile.

My flirtations are rewarded by a burst of color across her cheeks. It runs down her neck to the top of her simple navy dress. "Synthea," she repeats after taking a small sip of water. Her pert nose wrinkles, and her eyebrows scrunch together. "That's not very intimidating for a demon."

A loud chuckle bursts from my mouth. The sound has the beautiful stranger's lips curving into a wide grin, revealing twin dimples on either cheek. They suit the air of innocence she exudes.

An innocence I can't help but want to sully with my teeth and tongue. After all, that's what a demon does, right?

"No. It's not... But I think the horns and tail make up for it. Wouldn't you agree?" When the aforementioned tail slithers around my waist, the spade-shaped tip resting on the exposed sliver of gray skin between the bottom of my cropped tee and the top of my leather pants, her eyes widen.

Not in fear. No, her body language tells a different story. Elbows resting on the bar top, she leans closer, bright eyes caressing over every inch of me and lingering on the tattoos on my arms when I brace my hands on the bar. "They definitely do," she whispers.

Triceps flexing, I lean closer, drawn to her as though I'm a poor moth fluttering around a glowing flame. Sparks of sexual chemistry whir in the air between us like fireflies dancing in the night sky.

Before I can say "fuck it," throw her over my shoulder, and teleport us to my apartment, the stranger's eyes slam shut.

She shakes her head and leans back on her stool, obliterating the moment we just shared.

Does devastation fill my chest? Yes. But I clear my throat and brush it off, focusing instead on the fact that I still don't know her name. We need to remedy that situation ASAP. "Anyway, most people call me Syn. Hence, Synful Taproom." I wave a hand at the neon purple sign centered on the mirror behind the bar. "And you are?"

She extends a hand, and I don't miss the slight tremble in it. "Where are my manners? I'm Penelope."

Penelope. A beautiful name suited perfectly for someone with such alluring beauty.

When I grip her small hand in mine, that familiar heat zips up my arm again. Is she who I've been looking for since I came topside?

She doesn't display any outward signs of being a supernatural creature, like me. Rambling on about a mate bond two seconds after meeting would have any normal human running for the hills.

Does she even have experience with other monsters? Kind of hard not to when we're spilling from every crack and crevice in New York City now that we're out of hiding.

Let things progress naturally, Syn. If it's meant to be, it will be.

"It's nice to officially meet you, Penelope." My dark-stained lips peel into a smile, revealing the sharp points of my teeth.

Once again, Penelope's reaction isn't what I expect. Cheeks flushed, heat flares in her eyes. Absorbing most of the breathtaking blue, her pupils blow wide as they linger on my mouth, but she cuts the moment short *again.*

Gaze dropping to the bar top, her finger drags down the side of her glass. "I'm sorry about earlier. I don't know what came over me, but I'm sorry I caused a scene." Her eyes finally lift to mine, any trace of lust replaced with sincerity.

"Don't sweat it, sweetness." I chuckle before adding, "Chad McFuckface must have deserved it for a sugary sweet thing like you to throw her drink on him."

I'm graced by those adorable dimples again when she smiles, but her mouth quickly drops into a frown.

"You wanna tell me what happened?"

A gusted breath leaves her mouth. "Not really."

My lips curl over my teeth as I stifle a laugh and contemplate my next move. Finally, I land on, "I'm a really good listener. Promise." Extending my hand between us, I stick out my pinky. I need another hit of her skin against mine, no matter how small.

Her dimples reappear as she links her pinky with mine.

"I'm almost thirty." Penelope sighs, fingers going back to the damp side of her glass, drawing abstract designs in the condensation. Nervous energy fills her aura in murky waves.

I lean my hip against the bar and cross my arms over my chest. "Okay?"

"I guess that means my biological clock is about to stop ticking. At least that's what my mom thinks. So she's been setting me up on dates for the past few months. But the men are *awful*, each one worse than the last. All they want is Holly Homemaker to dote on them and pop out babies. That's not me. That's not the life I want."

My eyebrows draw together. "Have you told your mom any of this?"

Penelope's shoulders deflate. She's so small, so broken. I wish I could pull her into my lap and curl my shadows around her to shield her from the world.

"I've tried. Trust me. She doesn't listen. She's controlled my entire life to some extent." On the bar top, Penelope's phone screen lights up as it skitters against the shiny wood. "Speak of the devil." She declines the call and turns it screen down, only for it to start buzzing again. "I'm sure she's already heard about my little tantrum from Matthew or his mother."

"Do you need to get that?"

She finishes the last of her water in one gulp before shaking her head. "Enough trauma dumping. I'd rather enjoy the rest of my night with my new friend." A winning smile lights up her face. "Will you have a drink with me?"

"Yo! Syn!" a deep voice shouts from the opposite end of the bar and draws my attention away from Penelope. "Can we get another round?" A group of orcs occupy the stools, eyes glued to the television mounted on the wall. They're regulars. Every Thursday, they come to watch baseball or football or hockey… whatever happens to be on. They tip well and never cause problems.

Swinging my gaze back to Penelope, who I'm dying to spend more time with, I pat her forearm and say, "Gimme a few, sweetness, then we'll have that drink."

After helping the orc and his friends, I get sidetracked by several other customers. My shadows swirl around me, grabbing glasses, limes, and booze bottles, but my gaze stays glued to Penelope. The glow from her phone screen illuminates her face while her finger swipes, no doubt doom-scrolling some social media site.

Cool liquid hits my hand. "Fuck." Beer spills from the overflowing glass onto my fingers, drenching them. I switch off the tap and dump out the excess before sliding the glass across the bar to the customer.

Irritation ripples through me as I grab a rag and clean up my mess. *Where the hell is Rafe?* My eyes swing over my shoulder to the clock on the wall. His shift started ten minutes ago.

Thursday nights are surprisingly busy. People celebrating the gateway to the weekend and whatnot, I'm not really sure, but I always have extra waitstaff and a second bartender scheduled so we don't get behind.

"I'm late. I know." *Ladies and gents, here he is now!* "Sorry, boss," my pixie bartender mutters as he sidles up next to me, tying his apron around his waist. "The train was late, so I had to grab a cab."

I toss the beer-soaked rag into the bin under the bar, then slap Rafe on the back. He stands a few inches shorter than me, but his glittering navy wings more than make up for the height difference. "Don't sweat it, kid. You're here now; that's what matters. Can you handle things for a bit?" I tip my chin toward Penelope, who's still scrolling on her phone. "I promised someone a drink."

A smug grin stretches across Rafe's mouth, accentuating the snakebite piercings beneath his bottom lip. "Don't do anything I wouldn't do." He tosses me a wink as I brush off his words in favor of the sweet woman occupying the last seat at my bar.

"How about that drink?" I say, sliding two empty glasses between me and Penelope. "What's your poison?" But the smile on my lips falls when she shoves her phone into her purse and slides the strap over her shoulder.

What? She can't leave yet. I don't know anything about her.

"Sorry. I need to get home. Early meeting in the morning. But thank you—"

"How are you getting home?"

Penelope's eyes widen, throat tightening as she swallows. "Oh, umm. It's only a few blocks. I was going to walk—"

Not on my watch. "I can take you home. Call me old-fashioned, but I don't like the idea of you walking the city alone at night, and I won't be able to sleep until I know you're safe at home."

Coming on a little strong, aren't ya?

I clear my throat and add, "Plus, that douchecanoe could be waiting outside your place."

"Oh, umm." Her eyes ping-pong between me, Rafe, and the rest of the bar. "I didn't think of that."

The rush of customers seems to have died down since Rafe got here. *Lucky bastard*. He walks over to where I stand, wiping his hands on a rag. "You want me to start on inventory now that things have slowed down?"

"Nah, I've got it covered in the morning. But I do need you to hold down the fort while I get Penelope home."

Rafe's gaze shifts to Penelope, and the urge to gouge his eyeballs from his head surges through me. *Okay, what the fuck was that?*

I really didn't like that trust fund jackass's eyes on Penelope, but Rafe is my employee, my friend. Why the sudden possessiveness?

Before my thoughts spiral any further, a soft voice from across the bar grabs my attention. "How do I know I can trust you? We just met." Dismissal laces her tone when she says, "I'm just going to grab a cab."

I widen my eyes at Rafe and tip my head, hoping he gets the hint that I don't want Penelope leaving alone.

"Penelope?" He extends a hand to her, and somehow, I manage not to rip off his arm when her fingers grip his. "I'm Rafe. Listen, I've worked for Syn for... ten years. And she's only ever had my best interests at heart. If she's worried about you getting home safe, it's with good reason. Take the ride, darlin'."

Penelope gulps, and her eyes slide to mine. "Okay."

"I'll be back to help close up," I say to Rafe before telling Penelope, "Wait here." Then I dip into my office to grab my leather jacket, keys, and two helmets.

Chapter 3

Synthea

"I've never ridden on a motorcycle before," Penelope says once we're outside, eyeing my black sport bike like it might come to life and bite her. Pain pricks my tongue as I sink my sharp teeth into the muscle to stifle my laughter at her narrowed gaze.

Like always, my baby is parked in the reserved spot in front of the bar. My regular patrons know to leave it the fuck alone, and any strangers who don't... Well, they learn quickly that you don't mess with a demon's bike.

Taking Penelope's purse from her outstretched hand, I place it in the small compartment under the seat. "First time for everything. Right, sweetness?"

She takes the helmet from me and slips it on. "I guess so," she says through the open visor.

"Just hold on tight, lean when I do, and you'll be fine." I grab her hand to steady her as she swings her leg over the bike.

Raising her legs, she places her feet on the footpegs. The motion has the navy fabric of her dress sliding up to reveal tan, muscular thighs. *Fuck*. I nearly swallow my tongue, shoving my own helmet on to hide any drool leaking from my mouth.

What would it be like to drag my tongue across her skin? Would she mind the piercing I have there? Would it make her shiver with desire?

Before my thoughts can drive me to do something I'd regret—or not—I zip up my jacket and swing my leg over the bike, careful not to kick Penelope in the process.

Once I'm settled in front of her, she wraps her arms around my waist. Her grip is loose and hesitant.

Grabbing her hands in mine, I slide them under my jacket and lay her palms against my stomach, the thin fabric of my t-shirt the only barrier between us. "Gotta hang on tight, pretty girl." I tremble as she curls her fingers into my shirt, the warmth of her hands soaking through and into my skin.

I don't want tonight to be over. I don't want to drop her off at home.

But I also don't want to come off like a creep or a stalker. How do I make sure I see this woman again... and not just in my dreams?

"Ready?" I thread the key into the ignition.

Penelope's helmet clunks against mine when she nods. A soft "yes" follows close behind.

Cranking the key, the engine roars to life, vibrating between my thighs.

The purring power of the bike beneath me... It's right up there with the release of a good orgasm, and it never gets old.

I zip into traffic, cutting off a taxi in the process. "Watch where you're fucking going?" the driver shouts before laying on the horn.

Laughter fills my helmet. Behind me, Pen squeals and grips me tighter as I weave between cars.

She told me her address before we left the bar. It's only a few blocks away, but I'm planning to take the scenic route and savor every second with her arms wrapped around me, which is why I speed off in the opposite direction of her neighborhood.

A desperate chill fills the air as the wind whips around us, forcing Penelope to huddle closer. Headlights from oncoming traffic blur as we jet through the darkness and make it out of the bustling heart of the city.

One bad thing about riding a motorcycle: small talk is next to impossible. Even though I can bask in the warmth of Penelope's arms around me, I can't learn anything about her. I can't observe all the little nuances of her expression as she talks.

I'll plan better next time.

Because there will be a next time.

All too soon, we pull up to the curb in front of Penelope's apartment building.

I don't like what I find as I switch the engine off and my booted foot lands on the ground.

The broken streetlight on the sidewalk does a piss-poor job of illuminating anything, let alone a safe path to the front door of the building. Fallen from the building's facade, crumbling bricks, along with trash and cigarette butts, litter the pitted and cracked sidewalk.

A siren blares, red and blue lights zipping past us as I help Penelope off my bike and return her purse.

Surely, I took a wrong turn somewhere. This shithole can't be where my sweetness lives.

"Is this the right place?" I ask once we've removed our helmets. My gut tightens as I wait for her response.

Penelope's fingers fidget with the front of her cardigan, but pride blazes in her cerulean eyes when they lift to mine. "It's not much, but it's mine."

A long shadow stretches across the sidewalk from my left. On instinct, I step in front of Penelope and turn to face the assailant.

Face shrouded by a worn hood, the large figure approaches. My upper lip peels back to expose my sharp teeth, and a menacing growl shakes my body. Rolling my shoulders back, I make myself appear taller than my five-foot-ten stature.

Delicate fingers wrap around the clenched fist at my side. “Hey, it’s okay.” She steps around me, putting herself between me and the stranger. Bold or stupid, I’m not sure yet.

My arm shoots out, wrapping around her narrow waist and pulling her to my body. The heat radiating from her calms the beast who’s ready to rip this stranger limb from limb.

“Hi, Frank. No room at the shelter tonight?” There’s a friendliness to Penelope’s words. A pleasantness only reserved for someone you care about.

The stranger steps forward. Cast in the dim glow of the shitty broken streetlight, I finally get a look at him. Tired eyes meet mine. Sunken cheekbones give way to an unkempt, long beard. Holes mar the fabric of his threadbare hoodie and stained jeans. “’Fraid not, honey.”

Breaking out of my hold, Penelope pulls some bills from her purse before stopping in front of the man. Her free hand grips his forearm, and she slips the money into his palm as she murmurs, “For tomorrow. So you can get some food.”

"Bless you, Penelope." Pocketing the cash, he wraps her in a gentle one-armed hug before disappearing into the dark alleyway next to her building.

I erase the distance between us, falling in step with Penelope as she walks to the front door. The flimsy glass isn't as secure as I'd like, but the double lock and additional security door inside the entryway cool my boiling blood, just a smidge. "You shouldn't be handing out money to strangers, sweetness. Especially not at night."

Eyebrows at her hairline, she spins to face me. "Frank? Oh, he's not a stranger. He lived in the apartment next door to mine until he lost his job and couldn't make rent. He's a good guy… He just fell on hard times." Her keys jingle as she pulls them from her purse and faces the door again. "Everyone needs a little help now and again, Syn. I'm in a position to offer him that little boost, so I do."

Fuck, she really is an angel fallen from Heaven. I don't deserve to lick the motor oil-stained sidewalk at her feet.

This woman's heart is made of pure gold, and she's surely too good to be seen with the likes of me. But demons are known for being selfish and taking what they desire. Right now, I desire my sweet little human more than anything else.

"Thank you for giving me a ride. You really didn't have to inconvenience yourself for me," she says, wiggling her key into the lock and jiggling the handle.

I lean against the door when she swings it open, towering over her as she peers up with big, bright eyes. The need to touch her again wins out, hooking a finger under her chin, I keep her brilliant gaze on me. Leaning in until our breath mingles, seductive command oozes from my words. "Next time you've got a date, come to the Taproom, and I'll intervene if they're an asshat. You got it, sweetness?"

Blunt teeth sink into her bottom lip, her eyes going slightly glassy as they linger on my smirk. She nods, chin still clutched in my grip. Her hot breath fans my face when she whispers, "Got it. Goodnight, Syn." Then she slips from my grasp, *yet again*, opening the inner security door and disappearing up the stairs.

"Goodnight, sweetness. Until we meet again." Because we will. Of that, I'm absolutely certain... even though I was too enamored to get her phone number. *Fuck*. At least I know where she lives. I'll camp outside her door if that's what it takes to see her again.

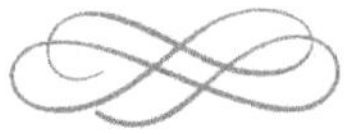

Marker in hand, I place a checkmark on my inventory list before moving on to the next item. After dropping Penelope off last night, my body was like a live wire, surging with pent-up electricity. What better way to release said energy than a moonlit ride along the river?

By the time I made it home, the horizon was blushed red by the rising sun. I managed to grab a few hours of shuteye before my alarm went off, reminding me it's inventory day at the Taproom.

A loud, grizzly sigh from behind me has me spinning on my booted heels. My hellhound guard, Fenrir, lays in his dog bed that I dragged out to the main bar area from my office. Sunbeams spill through the windows, making his sleek black fur shine. Blood-red eyes track my every move as I bounce from one shelf to the next, liquor bottles smooth beneath my fingertips as I count them.

After scribbling a checkmark in the vodka column, I glare at him over my shoulder. "Don't start with me. I already told you: you're staying here. I don't need your big, hairy ass frightening the poor realtor."

I can only imagine waltzing into the property across the street with a hellhound lumbering in after. The realtor would run away screaming, and I'd probably be blacklisted by Bauer Enterprises.

The size of a large wolf, Fen is much more menacing with his razor-sharp claws and teeth. Matching the obsidian color of his fur, a row of spikes lines his back, all the way to the tip of his tail. Fenrir huffs again, luminous eyes rolling when he crosses one giant paw over the other.

Of course, I had to be saddled with a hellhound whose attitude is bigger than he is, which is sayin' something.

I wag a finger at him, scolding him like a petulant child, which he pretty much is. "Don't roll your eyes at me, asshole. *You* volunteered for this assignment, remember?"

"I thought there would be more smiting and less domesticity, Princess." His gruff voice fills my head. In instances such as ours, where a hellhound is bound to a demon, they can communicate telepathically.

"Don't call me that." I hiss at the royal title, something I've spent the last fifty years running from.

"But I'm bored," he whines, widening his eyes until a sliver of white shows around the red. Puppy eyes, great.

"You could always—oh, I don't know—go back to Hell. No one's stopping you." Taking my turn as the petulant one, I stick out my tongue at him before turning to continue my inventory.

"That's not how it works, Princess. We're bound for eternity now. Plus, I like the sunshine. And the frozen sugar milk in an edible chalice." His tongue lolls out the side of his mouth, leaking a steady trail of drool onto the shiny tile below.

Great. I'll have to mop the floors again before opening.

Choosing to ignore his use of my title again, I giggle, honest to Satan, giggle. "You mean ice cream? Who gave you ice cream?" I turn again, arching an eyebrow at Fenrir.

"A true soldier never betrays his brethren."

Shaking my head, I resume counting the bottles of whiskey. I'd bet my coveted motorcycle that it was Xavier, my wolven bouncer. The male has a sweet tooth a mile wide and not a lick of self-control.

A familiar crackling hiss and the distinct odor of sulfur have me sighing as I set down my clipboard and marker. It's too early for this shit. "I already told you, Lucie. I'm done."

When I turn around, my sister stands on the other side of the bar, adjusting the pointed shoulders of her sleek blazer. The fabric hugs her large breasts and slim waist. She flips her long, black hair behind her back, dark eyes settling on me. "I don't see what's so great up here." Bathed in crimson, her lips pinch into a scowl.

"Well, if you ask Fenrir, it's the ice cream." The joke is lost on my sister as she turns to glare at the snoozing hellhound.

Half-sister, technically speaking. We share the same father, but my mother was human.

"You wouldn't understand," I say, interrupting the silence that's shrouded us. Rounding the bar, I come to stand in front of her and cross my arms over my chest, shielding myself from her scrutiny. "You've spent your whole life in Hell, but I can't do it. I gave you 200 years—like we agreed. Now I'm going to do what I want."

Her claw-tipped finger runs across the table beside her. She brings it to her face, inspecting it. I wiped down every surface in this place after closing last night, so there's no way she's found anything to match the disgusted look on her face. "Like running a dive bar? Because that's such a noble cause, Syn?"

She doesn't get it. The piece of my soul that's missing. The craving for companionship that's not normal for a demon. "It's not just that."

"Then what is it?" Her perfectly sculpted black eyebrow lifts with judgmental curiosity.

"I want sunlight and fresh air." Maybe I'm more like Fenrir than I care to admit. "And... *love*!"

She gags, recoiling. "Love?"

"Yeah," I croak. "I want to share my life with someone." When I originally left Hell, I told her I needed a change of scenery, but the more time I spent around mated pairs (human and monster), the more I craved what they had.

Lucie's eyebrows draw down, creasing in the middle, and she takes a seat on a stool at the bar. "But that's not what demons do. We were created for a purpose, to run the pits of Hell and keep order in the underworld. We don't belong up here, and we certainly don't do love. Sex... sure, but not *love*." Distaste sours her features when she spits the word, like it physically pains her to say.

"Maybe *you* don't, but *I* do." My gaze drops as I whisper the next part. "At least, I want to try."

"You're more like him than I thought." Her lip curls into a sneer when she refers to our father, who once ruled Hell with an iron fist. That was before...

I shake my head to banish those thoughts. Keep them locked away, so I don't have to face the emotions they awaken.

"Is that so bad?" I meet Lucie's eyes again, surprised at the sincerity I find there.

For a hardened demon who doesn't believe in love, she's always shown me kindness and compassion. Treated me like a true sister and not some half-blood bastard, but after she took her place as queen, she turned icy, and we grew distant. "I just don't want anyone to hurt you, Syn. Least of all for you to fall for a human." A shudder rolls down her spine. "If you open yourself up, like he did..." She shakes her head, no doubt banishing the memories of a darker time. "Come back home, and I can protect you. Wouldn't you be happier with a blade in your hand and a damned soul on your rack?"

Nausea rising, my stomach twists at the picture she paints. Call me weak, but torturing souls was never my thing. "I'm not having this argument with you again, Lucie. We've been going back and forth for half a century, to no avail." I sweep an arm around the Taproom. "This is my life now. If you can't accept that, then maybe you're not the sister I thought you were."

Dark eyes roll. "Always so sensitive. Don't come crying to me when someone rips your heart out and stomps all over it, dear sister. I'm liable to chain them to my rack for the rest of eternity." Her painted lips curve into a sinister smirk, revealing two rows of sharp teeth that are identical to mine.

"Wouldn't dream of it."

"Anyway," she says, standing from her stool and brushing a hand down her fitted black trousers. "The gates are always open if you change your mind. You know where to find them." A parting wink, and she bursts into flame, leaving behind a plume of smoke and another burst of sulfur.

Lucie probably thinks persuading me back to Hell is in my best interest, but it's not. It's in hers. Another loyal soldier. Another mindless demon to follow orders.

That's never been me. And it wasn't her, either... not until Dad died and she had to take his place.

"The audacity," I grumble, picking up my clipboard as I round the bar again. My nail clinks against the glass bottles as I count, soothing my insides after yet another tiff with Lucie.

How do I show her what being part of this world—this community—means to me? How it's given me more happiness than living in Hell ever did.

Chapter 4

"Are you ready?" Antoinette clutches her mug between her hands and leans her hip against my desk. Black scales shimmer under the morning sun as she brings the steaming beverage to her mouth and takes a sip.

If I had to guess, the bright purple mug is filled to the brim with lavender chamomile tea.

Antoinette is a dragon shifter, so she can be a bit prickly and short-tempered.

My fingers clack on my keyboard, adding a finishing flourish to my email before I hit send. I spin to face my boss, and friend. "As I'll ever be." My lips curl into a forced smile as I gulp down a swarming beehive of nerves. It settles in my stomach, buzzing until I think my breakfast might make an unwanted appearance.

Today is my first solo showing.

Claw-tipped fingers wrap around my hands, where they fidget with a pen. "You're going to be great, Pen. How many showings have you shadowed me and Cyrus on?" Her smile is a cool balm on my roiling tummy.

"Too many to count."

"Exactly! And when we were at Big York... you were doing half this stuff anyway. You're a natural."

After a disastrous falling out with our old boss, Antoinette started her own commercial real estate firm with her human mate, Cyrus. I tagged along for the ride, continuing to act as her assistant for the past few years, until she offered to help me get certified as an agent.

Taking the leap meant more money... but also, more responsibility. No longer could I just be a wallflower, taking orders from the boss. No, it meant forging my own path, something that was terrifying... yet exciting.

She pats my hand before standing. "I'm proud of you, Pen."

"Yeah, yeah." I wave her off. "I was wasting my potential. Blah. Blah. Blah."

"It's the truth," Cyrus says as he sweeps into our shared workspace. After being forced to share an office with Antoinette, his arch nemesis at the time, they decided to keep a similar atmosphere when opening Bauer Enterprises.

Minus the hostility and sexual tension. "I don't think we would've closed half the sales we did without you. And have I mentioned how amazing our website looks?" His wink has my cheeks heating, and I fight the urge to fan myself.

I'm not the best at taking compliments. Mostly, they make me all hot and itchy… and massively uncomfortable.

"Almost like it was designed by a professional," Annie adds while she takes a seat at her desk.

"It does look pretty good, doesn't it?" I mumble, praying my neck and chest haven't flushed bright red like my cheeks.

"Anyway, how was your date last night?" It's Cyrus who asks, catching me off guard. Why would he care about my love life?

"Oh, ummm." I busy my hands again, shuffling papers and checking my phone. "Not great." With a wince, I rush out the next part. "I might have dumped my drink on him… on purpose."

A loud burst of masculine laughter has my eyes slicing up from my desk. Cyrus slaps a hand over his mouth to stifle his chuckle while Annie glares at him. The next second, she's across our office and perched on the corner of my desk again.

Serious golden eyes scan my face. "What happened?"

Where do I start? Oh, my mom doesn't understand me at all and set me up with a misogynistic asshole. A gusted sigh leaves my mouth, and I lean back in my chair. "I don't know. He made a sexist remark—which I'd normally ignore—but something snapped in me."

"So you dumped your drink on him? Wish I could've been there to see it. Bet he deserved it." Humor lingers in Cyrus's deep voice.

"He did!" Unable to help it, a laugh spills from my mouth as I remember how absolutely *fuming* Matthew was. "It's not that I don't want to be with someone... But I don't want to be with someone who wants to shove me in the kitchen and take away my rights. Ya know?"

Annie nods. "You'll know when the right soul finds you, Pen." Her eyes lift to Cyrus, a soft pink coloring her cheekbones when he winks.

They may have had a rocky start, but I'd give anything to find a supportive partnership like theirs.

Maybe I've already found it... or should I say *her*?

My phone chimes, stopping any daydreams about the demon from last night. I doubt she'd even remember me this morning. She must get hundreds of patrons in her bar, and I'm nothing special.

Shaking my head, I clear the errant thoughts before silencing my calendar notification. I grab my bag and stand. "Any last words of advice?" My head swings between my bosses.

"Hellfyre, Inc. is a repeat customer, so it's a guaranteed home run, Pen. Just be yourself and you'll knock 'em dead," Annie says, patting my back as I head out the door.

My hand quakes as I slip the key into the lock and press the door open. After flipping on the lights, I smooth a hand over my ponytail, ensuring every hair is in place.

The walk over here did nothing to calm the butterflies in my gut. "It's going to be fine," I reassure myself as the lights flicker to life, spreading their warmth across the small storefront.

Abandoned for some time, Annie swooped it up, then replaced the flooring and light fixtures, before listing it for sale. Now it's a blank slate, ready for a new owner to mold it into something extraordinary.

Just be yourself and you'll knock 'em dead, Annie's words play in my mind, the pep talk I didn't know I needed.

I blow out a ragged breath, then shake my arms to release the tension and any lingering jitters. "You've got this, Pen." Walking back to the window, I peer through the spotless glass in hopes of spotting the client.

Purple neon across the way snags my attention and sends my heart into a tailspin. Embellished with a pair of horns and a pointed tail, Synful Taproom is illuminated, like a beacon in the darkness... or a reminder of the beautiful demon I met last night.

With her, my body lit up in a way I've never experienced before. Her presence had a calm washing over me that finally allowed my brain to shut off for just a little while. I wasn't worried about meeting my mom's unrealistic expectations, or the unrelenting nerves about the showing today.

I just *was*. Existing in her aura like it's where I belonged for eternity.

Maybe I'll swing by on my way back to the office and see if she's there. "Wait, *what*?"

Turning away from the window, I wipe my clammy hands on my pencil skirt. I'm not attracted to her... am I?

The steady click of my heels on the floor follows me as I pace, thoughts spiraling.

It's been shoved down my throat my entire life that I'm straight. That I should marry a man.

Being with a woman isn't an option. Not unless I want to cause a rift between my parents and be disowned by my mom.

Would it be so bad if she cut me out?

"Of course it would," I hiss. What if Dad and Colin followed her lead? I'd lose my entire family.

"Are you stalking me, sweetness?" the sultry voice purrs from behind me, snapping me back to the present.

Spinning to face the door, I find the very woman from last night. Lava erupts in my core at the sight of her.

Back braced against the open door, her strong arms are crossed over her vest-covered chest. The midmorning sun casts her in a golden glow, and my eyes are drawn to the double set of horns that arch from the top of her head. An inner set climbs toward the top of the doorframe, while the smaller set above her ears—that I hadn't noticed last night—lays close to her scalp.

Hair styled in loose waves and parted in the middle, hiding the shaved side, Syn is dressed in a fitted double-breasted vest and slacks. Both black, of course.

Corporate goth chic isn't a vibe I knew I was attracted to, but here we are.

She looks completely different from how she did last night. Polished. Professional. But I know it's her; the glowing gold ink on her toned arms and her uniquely feline eyes give her away.

My mouth snaps shut. I'm not really sure when it opened. "W-What? Me? No! Why would I—" Eyes wide, I wring my hands in front of me as she leaves her perch in the doorway.

Black motorcycle boots eat up the space between us until she's only a foot away. "Oh! You're even more adorable when you're flustered."

Right on cue, my cheeks flame, making her dark lips widen into a smirk. My eyes fall closed, and I force out a breath, willing the redness on my face to evaporate by the time my lids open again.

It's no use. I've always gotten flustered and tongue-tied under the smallest inconvenience.

Why does it have to be right now? Right before I'm due to meet with a client.

Fisting my hands at my sides, I suck in a cleansing breath through my nostrils. Instead of reducing my anxiety, the scents of sugary sweet cherries and rich bourbon surround me when I fill my lungs.

"Penelope? Are you okay? I didn't mean to upset you." A soft hand cups my burning cheek, and my eyes flutter open.

She's right there.

In my space.

Eyes roaming, I eat up every inch, every detail, of her face that I missed last night. Pointed ears are lined with gold hoops and glittering stud earrings. Two more hoops bisect her right eyebrow, which, like its partner, is crouched low over her dark eyes. The almond shape is accentuated by a dark flick of eyeliner at the outer corner of each.

Reaching up, I smooth a finger between her eyebrows until they relax. "I'm alright," I whisper. "I wasn't expecting to see you, is all."

I should stop my perusal of her face and put some space between us. But I don't.

I can't.

And she doesn't seem to want me to stop either. Thumb caressing my cheek, Syn leans closer. Her nose is somehow strong, yet delicate, a direct contradiction, just like her monstrous beauty. One nostril bears a simple golden hoop that matches the pair in her eyebrow.

A purple gemstone above her Cupid's bow has my eyes dragging down to her lush, full lips. They're a dark purplish-mauve, and I'm not sure if it's lipstick or their natural color. What would they feel like on mine?

What? The thought triggers my brain to come back online, and I slip out of her embrace, putting much needed space between us.

I've never been so awestruck and caught off guard by someone before. The sexual tension between us is off the charts. Clearing my throat—and my head—yet again, I ask, "What are you doing here?"

"I scheduled a showing with the listing agent."

My eyebrows shoot up. "That's me," I squeak. "Wait, *you're* S. Hellfyre?"

Sharp teeth make an appearance when she smiles, waving a hand from her curved horns to the clunky boots on her feet. "In the flesh, sweetness."

Try as I may, I can't stop the tremble that works down my spine at the nickname. She used it several times last night, too.

As if she can sense my inner turmoil, Syn spins in a slow circle, eyes assessing the empty space around us. Finally facing me again, her smile is gentle and her voice is soft. “So… how about that showing?”

“Right. Yes.” I smooth my hands down the front of my tight skirt, letting the sleek fabric ground me. Then I roll my shoulders back. *I can do this.* Launching into the rehearsed informational speech I prepared, I bombard her with facts and tidbits about the space for the next few minutes. Syn trails behind me, but leaves an appropriate amount of space between us. Nodding along, she’s quiet, like she’s deep in thought as her eyes rake over every detail.

In turn, my eyes do some wandering of their own, specifically to Syn’s arms. Gold ink shimmers and sparkles like fine diamonds against the canvas of her gray skin. Most of her right arm is taken up by a large snake. It wraps around the toned muscles of her bicep and forearm, with the head resting on the back of her hand.

She has really beautiful arms. Should I tell her? That’d be weird… right?

Shaking my head, I give Syn a few minutes of quiet to look over the space. The silence lets me finish my perusal of her tattoos. The snake’s mouth is open wide with ferocious fangs dripping venom.

Surrounded by delicate flowers and realistic macabre skulls, I’m surprised it hasn’t slithered from her skin and sunk those menacing fangs into me. I stifle the tremble that threatens to shake my spine. Why do I like the idea of her sharp teeth on my skin?

"Are you looking to expand the Taproom?" I ask, breaking the silence once we finish the tour. Although, it'd be strange to open a second location directly across the street.

She shakes her head. "Not quite. You remember Rafe?"

I nod, smiling at the memory of the flirty pixie. "The other bartender from last night."

"When he isn't working at the Taproom, he works as a tattoo artist. The shop he works for is..." She rubs her fingers along her jaw as she searches for the words. "Not great."

"So you're buying him a shop?" My eyebrows wing up.

Syn simply shrugs, like buying an entire building for an employee is normal. "I have money burning a hole in my pocket, and it's been a while since I acquired a new property. You'll find, Penelope, that I'd move Hell and Earth for those I care about." The intensity behind her onyx eyes has me gulping. "I'd like to make an offer."

"Oh... I mean, *yes*, of course." I'm caught off guard, still drowning in her gaze, and I fumble as I grab a business card from my bag. "Here's all of my contact information."

With a smile creasing the corners of her eyes, she snatches the card from my hand and holds it to her chest, like she's won some grand prize. "Perfect. I'll have my lawyer draw up the papers and send them your way. I think we'll be seeing a lot more of each other very soon, Penelope."

I can only hope.

The wink that accompanies her parting words has my stomach swooping once again.

Chapter 5

Synthea

It's been a few days since the showing with Penelope. Much to my chagrin, our only correspondence has been via email. But I have my in… and her phone number.

What are the odds that she was the selling agent for the property I had my eyes on?

Must be fate or something.

I haven't been able to get her out of my damn head either, preparing the wrong drink order more times than I can count or dropping glasses and having to start over. It's unlike me. I'm smooth, confident, but the sweet little blonde human has me in a tizzy.

Morning rays of sun warm my skin as Fenrir leads me down the sidewalk. My boots clomp against the cement as he tugs on his leash, nearly ripping it from my hand. "Would you slow down, you big brute? It's Sunday morning. Can't we just go for a leisurely stroll?"

Nose to the ground, he completely ignores me, and I'm helpless to follow as he leads me to who knows where. On the search for something sugary, I'm sure. *Stupid hellhound and his damn sweet tooth.*

Lush greenery of Central Park to my right, Fenrir turns toward 79th Street. So much for a quiet walk in the park to clear my head after it's been consumed by Penelope.

"Do you smell that?" Fenrir's voice interrupts my thoughts, excitement lifting it an octave higher than its usual growly baritone.

"No," I say as he drags me to a gathering of tents on the tree-lined street. The farmers' market. My lips tilt into a smile. Okay, maybe my stubborn hellhound hasn't ruined my morning quite yet.

It's still early. Only a handful of people mill around from booth to booth, browsing fresh produce and other goods. "Care to share with the rest of the class?"

"Sugar, vanilla..." His spine-laiden tail wags, nearly striking a woman as she passes us, and his slobbery pink tongue hangs out the side of his mouth.

A chain reaction of events happens in the next blink.

A rogue fly buzzes too close to my face and hits my eye. "Fuck!" I double over and slap a hand over my stinging eye. At that same moment, Fenrir sprints forward, and the leash slips from my fingers.

Gone like a literal hound out of Hell, a flash of black fur and spikes disappears between the booths.

"Damnit, Fenrir!" Through blurry vision in one eye and sun glare in the other, I charge after my impetuous companion.

Nearly face-planting into a table of fresh berries, I spin on my toes at the last minute in pursuit of Fenrir. I'm coming back for some of those juicy strawberries later... after I murder a centuries-old hellhound.

I round another row of booths before my boots come to a screeching halt on the pavement.

Leaned over Fenrir, who's slobbering all over the front of her skin-tight pink leggings, is none other than *Penelope Martin*.

Thanks to her giving me her business card the other day, I now know not only her last name and phone number, but that she works for Bauer Enterprises as a junior agent.

"Aren't you the sweetest? But where's your owner?" Linen tote bag draped over her arm, her delicate fingers scratch between his pointed ears.

And Fenrir? Well, he's lapping up every second of attention. Eyes pinched shut, his mouth is open and panting as a string of drool drips onto the sidewalk below.

Shoving my hands into the pockets of my black denim shorts, I whistle an upbeat tune as I stroll toward them. My pace is slow. Not wanting to break their little bubble yet, I lurk near the booth across the way.

Penelope runs a hand along Fenrir's back, avoiding the spikes on his spine. His butt wiggles as his tail slaps back and forth at a rate I've never witnessed before. He likes her... *a lot*. "You're wearing a leash, so you must belong to someone." Her hands look so small when her fingers sink into the fur on the sides of his neck, and she directs his eyes to her. "Can you be a good boy and help me find your owner?"

"You just going to stand there, Princess?" Fenrir taunts through our bond.

I swear the bastard winks before dragging his slobbering tongue up the side of Penelope's face, which causes an angel's chorus of giggles to spill from her mouth. The crisp, lyrical sound has me leaving the swathe of shadows I'm hiding in and making a beeline for them.

"You sure you're not stalking me, sweetness?" I say once I'm standing next to Fenrir.

"Syn!" Penelope's voice cracks when she says my name. "W-What are you doing here?"

Bending down, my fingers scrape the pavement when I grab his leash from the ground and slip it over my wrist. "We were out for a stroll when this one ran off." I tip my head toward my menace of a hellhound, who ignores me and nuzzles into her hand. "I see you've met Fenrir. Sorry about the drool."

Penelope's eyes widen to a comical size as they ping from me to Fenrir. Her mouth pops into a perfect 'O' shape. "H-He's yours?"

"Unfortunately. It's a long story."

"Did you smell her, Princess? She smells like those little moist cakes with the sugary paste on top."

Sucking in a breath, my nostrils flare, and an overwhelming sweet vanilla scent wafts off of Penelope. "Cupcakes, Fenrir, cupcakes," I correct him as he licks her hand.

"Right, cupcakes. She tastes like one, too. Can we eat her?"

I close my eyes and pinch the bridge of my nose, shaking my head. "No, Fenrir. You cannot eat Penelope."

Well, *you* can't, but maybe she'll let *me*.

My thoughts of tasting the sweet cupcake between Penelope's thighs are cut short when she squeaks, "What?!"

I smile, hoping to ease the tension. "We can communicate telepathically, and he says you taste and smell like a cupcake. He won't *actually* eat you." *At least, I hope not.* I'll snap his neck if he tries.

"Oh." She holds her fingers out, and Fenrir gives them another taste. "It's not cupcake. It's probably frosting from the cinnamon roll I had." She points over her shoulder to a bright pink booth with a flying saucer logo I'd recognize in my sleep.

"You're a fan of Cream Me Up?" I ask, referring to the diner run by a couple of my friends, Maria and Phil. He's an orc and she's a pixie.

Fenrir must have finished cleaning her fingers, because he lays at my feet as Penelope pulls out a small bottle of clear gel, dumps some on her hands, and rubs them together. "Ah, yeah. Who isn't?"

"True." Yet another reason she's perfect for me. I can picture it now… After a long, passionate night of rolling in the sheets, we could sleep in and share brunch together.

"Now, about this stalking business." She smirks. "I think *you're* the one who's stalking me," she says as she crosses her arms over her chest. The move draws my eyes to the tight sports bra she's wearing. It's the same light pink as her leggings and molds her small breasts into perfect, perky peaks.

Before I can stop it, my tongue drags across my bottom lip.

A gentle throat clearing has my gaze slicing up to Penelope's face. One corner of her mouth pulls into a crooked grin. "My eyes are up here, Syn." Fingers in a V, she points them at her baby blues.

Caught with my hand in the cookie jar.

Oops.

Do I feel bad? Not in the slightest. "Payback for the way you were leering at me the other day."

She splutters, so I add, "Don't think I didn't notice, sweetness."

A beautiful strawberry-red blush feathers her neck and cheeks. "You noticed that?"

Grabbing a bouquet of fresh flowers from the stand in front of us, I tuck it under my arm before pulling some cash from my pocket and handing it to the vendor. "Sure did, and I didn't mind one bit. Come on, looks like we've got some shopping to do." Heat licks the skin of my tail when it brushes up her arm.

Penelope shivers. Her pupils blow wide as they track the movement.

The subtle reaction urges me to continue my path, curling the tip of my tail around the straps of her empty tote bag. I give them a playful tug before letting my tail uncoil and slink behind me.

With a yank on the leash, I lead Fenrir back toward the strawberries I saw earlier, leaving Penelope behind with her mouth gaping.

Your move, sweetness.

Like I knew she would, Penelope eventually snapped her mouth shut and followed me to the next booth. I spent the morning bombarding her with questions, trying to learn as much about her as possible.

She has an older brother, who's married with two kids. She was raised in the Hamptons.

I devoured every little crumb she dropped, waiting like a good puppy for more.

Her favorite color is blue. Her favorite flowers are daisies.

Once her bag was full, I was the one following her as she headed toward her apartment.

"You really didn't have to buy these for me," Penelope says, holding the bouquet of vibrant blooms to her nose and inhaling. A soft moan leaves her plush lips.

But I did. In fact, any time she picked something up, shook her head, and set it back down, I slipped the vendor some cash and stuffed the item into her bag. The straps dig into my shoulder with how heavy the linen tote is.

Somewhere along the way, I ended up with Penelope's bag and she ended up with Fenrir's leash. Not that he seems to mind, trailing behind her to the front door of her apartment building, tail whipping from side to side.

"It's not a big deal." My opposite hand goes to the back of my neck, the skin unusually hot with… *nerves*? I clear my throat. "We should do this again sometime." My cheeks burn like a damn virgin. Why does sweet Penelope Martin have my stomach on the verge of falling out my ass?

A breathtaking smile lights up her whole face when she spins toward me, back braced against the crumbling brick of the building. "I'd really like that."

Drawn to her like a magnet, I step into her personal bubble. Neck arching, her head tips back, pupils blowing wide when I brace my hand above her head.

Kiss her, my brain screams, mouth lowering to hover mere inches from hers.

Penelope's tongue drags across her lush bottom lip, wetting the flesh and making it that much more appetizing. Her eyes close, and a whoosh of air leaves her nose, flaring her nostrils. A delicate hand lands on my chest, which is heaving like I can't catch my breath, applying enough pressure to make her intentions clear. "I should probably get inside. Thank you again for the flowers," she says in a soft voice.

As much as I don't want to, I respect her wishes and take a step back. I exchange the produce-filled tote for Fenrir's leash. "So I'll see you next Sunday?"

She's going to say no. I took things too fast and scared her.

Penelope digs her keys from her bag and unlocks the door. At the last minute, she peeks over her shoulder, a shy smile curling one corner of her mouth. "I'll meet you there."

It takes all my restraint not to pump my fist in the air and shout. That'd be weird. Tucking my hands into my pockets, I return her smile and nod. "See you there, sweetness." Then she disappears into the building, leaving me to calm the raging hoofbeats of my heart.

"You've got it bad, Princess." Fenrir's husky chuckle follows his words.

"One could say the same about you... Following her around like some lovesick pup," I chide as we amble down the sidewalk. I could teleport, but I need the fresh air and exercise to work through the jumbled mess in my brain.

Penelope likes me, but something's holding her back. What is it?

"I understand why you call her sweetness. She is exceptionally sweet for a tiny human."

"Yes, she is, indeed." And I was *this* close to finding out if her plump lips taste as sweet as I imagine.

Movement in the alleyway next to the building has my feet halting. My shadows uncoil from my body, ready to take on any danger.

Fenrir stops in front of me, the fur along his spine standing on end to surround the spikes that run down his back.

"You're that demon from the other night." The stranger's gruff voice precedes him as he emerges from the shadows of the alley. Same worn hoodie and jeans, it's the homeless man from the night I dropped Penelope off. What the fuck was his name? I was so focused on my sweetness that I can't remember.

Keeping hold of Fenrir's leash, I cross my arms over my chest and cock one hip. "Kind of creepy to be hiding in a dark alley, don't you think?"

The man shrugs. "Thought you were the cops."

"You in trouble with the law?"

He shakes his head. "No, but they don't take kindly to those who live on the streets."

Frank. His name hits me like a ton of bricks, along with an ingenious idea that should win me some brownie points with Penelope.

"Penelope seems to think you've hit a rough patch. You're not taking advantage of her, are you?" I arch an eyebrow at him, shadows swirling around me to make me appear larger than I am.

The man doesn't cower. To my surprise, he straightens his spine and rolls his shoulders back, something flashing in his eyes akin to courage. "I'm not that kind of man. Penelope is sweet, too sweet for this world, maybe a little naïve. Even after getting evicted, I stayed around to make sure no one hurt her."

Okay, so maybe he is a good guy.

Blowing out a sigh, I rub my fingers across my lips. *Fuck.* If I wasn't already head over heels for this woman, I'd leave this guy in the gutter to fend for himself. Apparently, falling for a sweet little human has me growing a conscience. "Frank, right?"

He nods.

"Here's what I can do for you, since Penelope seems to think you're a decent human who's down on his luck... You ever heard of the Synful Taproom?"

"Yeah, over on Crawford?"

"That's the one. I own the place. My dishwasher up and quit the other day, so I'm a little short staffed. Job's yours, if you want it. There's also a studio apartment that you can stay in until you get your feet under you."

Eyes pinched to slivers, he scrutinizes me. "Why would you help me?"

I shrug. "Seems Penelope's sweetness is wearing off on me. So here's the deal... Apartment is yours, rent free for two months. That should give you enough time to save up some cash. I expect you to show up on time to work and not fuck around while you're there. Can you do that?"

His head bobs up and down. "Yes, of course." Beneath the bruising under his eyes, sunken cheeks, and scruffy beard, it's hard to tell how old he is.

"Take my hand," I instruct, holding my palm out to him.

"Wha— Why?"

"Just do it!"

Jolted into action, his rough fingers curl around my palm. I close my eyes as flames engulf us. Darkness surrounds us, then a crack of lightning, and we're outside the door to the Taproom.

"Holy fuck!" Frank shouts, followed by the wet plop of him spewing the contents of his stomach on the sidewalk.

"First time teleporting?" I brush a stray speck of dust from my shoulder and step around him. "Sometimes it can be rough on your stomach."

Wiping the back of his hand over his mouth, he straightens. Green eyes glare at me. "A little warning would've been nice."

"Nah. It's like ripping off a bandage. Better to just get it over with," I say, pulling my key from my pocket. "Let me show you the apartment." I whip around at the last minute, pinning Frank with the full weight of my stare. "I'm taking a risk here. Don't make me regret it."

His throat clicks with a swallow, and he nods before following me and Fenrir inside.

"Risk it for the biscuit. Eh, Princess?" A hoarse, barking laugh comes from Fen's muzzle as I roll my eyes.

"Shut up, Fenrir!"

Chapter 6

Why did I think it was a good idea to come here after what happened on Sunday? My eyes swing around the bustling bar, searching for familiar purple hair.

My heart sinks when I don't find her. Maybe she's not here. *Or maybe she's ignoring you*, the little nagging voice at the back of my head chimes in.

Why would she ignore me? She was going to kiss me.

At least, I think she was.

And I think I wanted her to.

Syn exudes this sexuality and confidence that's addictive. I crave her energy more than I ever have with anyone else.

...But she's a woman.

Am I attracted to her in *that* way?

Does that make me a lesbian?

I like men.

Don't I?

My brain is a muddled mess, not getting any less murky since my last interaction with Syn.

"Earth to Pen." A hand waves in front of my face, and I blink to find my older brother's blue eyes narrowed with concern. "You okay?"

Like always, I plaster on a smile before picking up the menu and scanning its contents. "Yeah, fine. Just zoned out for a second."

My eyes flick up to find his brow crinkled, gaze lingering on my face like he doesn't believe a word coming out of my mouth.

"How are Jenn and the kids?" I ask, changing the subject before he can pester me. My thumbnail runs over the corner of the laminated paper as I wait for his response. We already ordered, but the waiter left the menus on the table, and I need something to keep my hands busy.

"They're good." A slow smile takes over his face, like it always does when he talks about his family. "Jenn is working a double at the hospital tonight, so Sam and Emory are with her parents. They missed Sam's birthday this year, so it's a belated celebration."

I nod and smile. "I can't believe he's already ten."

"Em will be eight this winter. I don't know where my babies went." He clears his throat and dabs the corner of his eye. One thing's for sure, my brother is a big ol' softie for his kids. Growing up with parents like ours didn't seem to impact his ability to be an amazing dad. "You'll have to come for the weekend soon. The kids miss Aunty Pen." My brother chuckles.

Besides Colin and Jenn, my niece and nephew are my favorite people in the world. I love spending the occasional weekend at their place in the suburbs, especially in the summer when I can take the kids to the beach or a movie.

"Things are busy at work right now. And I have a girls' weekend with Annie, Ness, and Maggie in a few weeks, but I should be able to fit in one more visit for my favorite niece and nephew."

He laughs at my lame joke, but the sound fades into silence as his expression sobers. "The new position at work isn't too much stress, is it? Any migraines lately?"

I swallow, eyes dropping to my menu again. Stress leads to migraines. And migraines lead to an uptick in my anxiety and depression. Overall, it's a recipe for disaster.

"Not in a few months. I'm trying to manage my stress levels. Annie's been great about not overwhelming me; plus, she's understanding if I have an attack and need time off."

Colin reaches across the table, fingers wrapping around my forearm. "I'm glad your boss is understanding. And you know Jenn and I are here if you need anything. Mom might be a bitch, but you have other family you can lean on. Okay, Pen?"

Unable to form words as tears well in my eyes and a lump clogs my throat, I simply nod.

I was a late bloomer, not starting my period until I was eighteen. And with it came excruciating and unpredictable migraines. *You're being dramatic, Penelope. There's nothing wrong with you*, Mom said when I told her, brushing off my complaints.

Dad was on a big case at the time, and working long hours, so I didn't want to bother him.

Instead, I went to the only other woman I trusted: my brother's girlfriend. Jenn was in her second year of nursing school. She got me an appointment with a neurologist to figure out what was happening. They diagnosed me with hemiplegic migraines with an aura and prescribed meds to manage when an attack happened.

At the time, I was a broke and slightly forgetful college student, so Colin and Jenn made sure I always had meds and a plan in case I had an attack. Without them, I wouldn't have gotten the help I needed.

"Speaking of Mom," I say, shoving aside the trauma of my late teen years. "Did I tell you about the date she set me up on last week?"

Colin's lips collapse into a scowl. "No. Why do you submit yourself to her torture, Pen?"

I shrug, not really sure how to explain to him that, even as I approach my thirties, I still don't want to disappoint her. For some twisted reason, I need her validation and approval. "I don't know. Maybe she's right? Maybe it's time for me to settle down?"

"Yeah, but not with one of those silver spoon misogynist—"

"Sweetness." The purr of her voice has my head snapping to the end of the booth. In all her glory, Syn stands with one hand braced on her hip and the other balancing a tray full of food and drinks. Sharp teeth peek out when her lips peel into a wide grin.

"Syn... uh, hi." My voice wobbles, and my tummy swoops.

Same as always, she's dressed from head to toe in black, the gray skin of her toned stomach on display beneath her cropped band tee. I gulp as my eyes skim up to her face, the smirk there growing wider.

Why does she have to be so sexy? The total opposite of little, awkward Penelope Martin?

Even if I were into women, she's millions of miles out of my league.

A plate hits the table, and she slides it in front of my brother, but her dark eyes stay on me. "Do I need to intervene, or is your date behaving?"

Half a fry clutched in his fingers, Colin chokes on a mouthful of food. Dropping the fry, he grabs his glass and takes a few gulps of water. When he sets it down again, his free hand curls into a fist and pounds on his chest as he coughs. "I'm sorry? Date?" His eyes swing from me to Syn, eyebrows rising.

Giggles burst from my mouth at the utter confusion written across his face.

Lifting my eyes to Syn again, she looks just as confused—if not more—than Colin.

Once my laughter has faded, I wave a hand across the table. "No violence necessary... this time. This is my brother, Colin."

Syn dips her chin. "Oh. Hi, Colin."

My brother lifts his hand in a small, pathetic wave. "Hi."

"And this is Syn..." I lift a hand in her direction, but sweat dampens the palm at my next words. "My friend."

Is that what she is? A friend?

Palpable sexual chemistry ripples between us every time we're together. We've almost kissed on more than one occasion. Is that normal for friends? I may not have a lot, but I assume friends don't almost kiss or look at you with bedroom eyes every time they see you.

I look up at Syn, hoping and praying her facial expression will lend me a clue, but her features are carved from stone, giving nothing away.

A quiet lull falls over the table, but she breaks it by saying, "Sure. If you call casually stalking me being my friend, then we're friends, sweetness." Her wink that follows is downright wicked, and based on her smirk, she knows it.

My skin heats, and I don't have the courage to face my brother.

"I'll be seeing you." Then she turns to Colin and says, "It was nice to meet you. Enjoy your burgers."

As much as I try, I can't drag my eyes away from the subtle sway of her narrow hips or the flick of her tail as she walks back to the bar.

Across the table, Colin clears his throat. When I manage to pull my gaze away from Syn, he's leaning against the burgundy velvet back of our booth, with his arms crossed over his chest. So help me, I want to wipe the stupid smirk right off his face.

Swiping a hand through his dark-blond hair, his blue eyes twinkle when he leans his elbows on the table. "Who was that, baby sister?"

"No one," I rush to say, not leaving a breath between his question and my response.

He shoves a fry into his mouth. "Mhm. Well, I'm here if you need someone to talk to."

It's on the tip of my tongue to spill my guts and tell Colin about how Syn and I keep running into each other, like an invisible string has tied our paths together.

Or how each encounter has lust blooming deep in my core.

Or how the anxious thoughts quiet to a dull hum when I'm in her presence.

Instead, I chicken out. "I know," I mumble before taking a bite of my bacon cheeseburger. Right now, my emotions are too muddled and confusing for me to process, so how would Colin be able to help?

Plus, what would he know about having an identity crisis?

I'll figure it out on my own.

Chapter 7

Could this day get any worse? I tug my keys from my purse as I trudge up the stairs to my apartment. Legs like cement, the journey takes every ounce of strength I have left. My second showing today went about as well as a screen door on a submarine. The man was extremely rude and borderline belligerent.

Somehow, I managed to keep the tears from falling until Annie showed up to rescue me.

She was able to smooth things over so we didn't lose a client, but we lost the sale, leaving me deflated. Even now, thoughts that I'm a failure run through my head as I make it to the third floor.

To make matters worse, there's a voicemail from Mom waiting on my phone.

I can only imagine what eligible suitor she's found for me this time.

After the debacle with Matthew, I managed to avoid her calls for a few days, so the "you've disappointed me" speech was short and did minimal damage to my psyche.

Ugh. I know I need to tell her to back off, but the weight of disappointing her settles on my chest, making it hard to breathe.

Leaning against the hallway wall, I close my eyes and fill my lungs before forcing them empty. Again and again, until the elephant kindly vacates his seat on my chest. My lids flutter open, and out of the corner of my eye, something small and fuzzy skitters across the stained carpet. A shriek rattles from my throat, and I plaster my back to the wall.

Is this the first time I've seen a rat in my building? No.

Are there also mysterious black spots on some of the walls and a suspicious odor in the basement laundry room? Yes.

But in a metropolis like New York City, housing doesn't come cheap, and this is the only place I could afford on my own.

Once I'm sure the little pest is gone, I continue to my apartment.

As if to add insult to injury, an ominous red paper is taped to my door.

The building is owned by some big corporation, so they usually communicate by leaving any important updates in our mailboxes. And since rent money is automatically withdrawn from my checking account, I know I'm not behind on payments.

My pulse thunders in my ears as I reach for the paper with numb fingertips. **Eviction Notice** is typed at the top in large, bold letters.

"This can't be happening." The flimsy paper shakes in my grip. The words swim across the page as I try to read them.

Infested.

Black mold.

Vacate immediately.

My stomach plummets.

I knew it wasn't the nicest building when I moved in, and maybe I was naïve in ignoring the obvious, but having to move out within twenty-four hours seems extreme.

A wavy line flashes across my vision. Moisture burns the backs of my eyes. *No. Not now. This can't be happening now.*

Panic grips my chest, shortening my breath.

It was only last week that I told Colin I've been migraine free for a few months. Guess my luck's run out.

Crumpling the eviction notice in one hand, I wiggle my key into the lock with the other. My shoulder collides with the door, shoving it open as I tumble into my apartment.

Dropping my bag on the worn countertop, shimmering lights in my periphery join the wavy lines.

Sweat dampens my palms when I fumble to open the kitchen cabinet where I keep my migraine medication. If I take them in time, maybe the attack will go away.

The familiar cardboard box is in my hand the next second, and I'm tearing open the foil pill packet. Slipping the little white disc under my tongue, sweet mint fills my mouth as it dissolves. Back braced against the counter, I fall to the floor, and the tears finally break free.

On a harsh sigh, I tip my head back and squeeze my eyes shut. "When it rains, it pours," I murmur into my empty apartment as the dominoes of my life come crashing down.

I'm not sure how long I sit on my kitchen floor, but when I peel my eyes open again, my vision is back to normal. The meds have kicked in, staving off the migraine aura... which is the scariest part. Not being able to see, having motor dysfunction, and feeling trapped in my own body.

No thanks.

The setting sun casts long, shadowy fingers across the peeling linoleum. Curling my hand around the edge of the counter, I use it as leverage to get to my feet. Every ounce of energy has been zapped from my body, and my limbs are heavy and weak as I search the cupboard for a clean glass.

Ah ha! Fingertips hooking over the lip of the cup, I drag it off the shelf, bring it to the sink, and fill it until it's nearly overflowing.

Cool water hits my tongue, and I could cry, but I think I used up all my tears earlier.

I chug not one, but two full glasses of water, before I pick up the red paper again.

This time, the words are clear.

Unfortunately, I wasn't imagining things and I am being evicted—effective immediately. No exceptions.

In fact, the letter explains, the entire building is being cleared out and condemned due to failing a city inspection.

Bracing my hands on the counter, I drop my head between my arms. "Where am I gonna go?"

Absolutely, under no circumstances, can I go home. I will not go back to living under my *mother's* thumb. Is she still controlling me to some extent? Sure, but I choose to be in denial about it for the time being.

I lean my hip against the counter and rub my temple. Colin and Jenn have their own busy lives; I don't want to burden them. Plus, they live too far outside the city for me to commute every day.

Annie and Cyrus are still in their honeymoon period as mates. I don't want to encroach on their bliss.

What about Syn? a little voice in the back of my head supplies.

"I can't."

You're kind of out of options, Pen.

I pull my phone from my purse. "I'll just call and see if she knows of any open apartments." The bright glow of my phone screen has my eyes burning, and I squint as my fingers navigate on autopilot. Somehow, I make it into my email inbox.

When I scroll to the bottom of the message, Hellfyre, Inc. stares back at me with a phone number listed underneath.

My thumb hovers over the digits. "Fuck it." Before I can overthink, I click the number and bring the phone to my ear.

Chapter 8

Synthea

The potent, hoppy smell tickles my nostrils as pale, frothy liquid pours into the glass and the carbonated bubbles hiss. Tail wrapped around the tap handle, I flick it off and grab a coaster, sliding the beer to the customer.

"Thanks, Syn," he says with a smile before placing a stack of bills on the bar top.

"Sure thing. Let me grab your change." I sweep the pile of cash into my hand, calling over my shoulder as I head to the register.

Rafe is already there, cashing out another order. "Where's your cute little blonde?"

"None of your beeswax, kid. Now, scoot." Avoiding his wings, I hip check him out of the way so I can get my customer his change.

Rafe, the asshole, smirks and chuckles as he walks away.

It's been five days since I last saw Penelope.

Yes, I'm counting. It's truly pathetic, but I can't get her out of my head.

When she didn't show up to the farmers' market on Sunday, it stung, but I'm not easily deterred.

I want her.

And I will have her.

Speaking of... my phone vibrates in my back pocket. A wide smile spreads across my lips when I pull it out. Penelope's name flashes across the screen, a sight that has my body practically floating like a hot-air balloon.

When Rafe walks past again, I shove the change into his hand and tip my head toward the customer. "Dude in the red jacket. I gotta take this call." Not waiting for his response, I make a beeline away from the boisterous conversation and laughter of the main bar and slip down the hall to my office.

Back braced against the door, I swipe to accept the call and bring the phone to my ear. "Sweetness," I purr. "And here I thought you were avoiding me."

A sniffle echoes down the line before a choked, "S-Syn."

My stomach plummets, bile climbing up my throat. "Baby girl, what's wrong? Where are you? Who do I need to hurt?"

Penelope sniffles again. "No one. I just..." She blows out a breath. "I'm bad at this. I-I think I need your help." The wobble in her voice tears a shred off my heart.

"Are you at home?"

"Umm. Y-Yeah."

"Say no more. See you in a sec, sweetness." I end the call before she can object.

Thank Satan it's Tuesday, which means things are slow. Popping back out to the bar, I spot Frank.

The man looks unrecognizable now that his beard is short and neat along his square jaw. Gone are the long, stringy locks; instead, his dark-brown hair is secured into a sleek bun.

"Frank." I call him over with a wave of my hand.

"Is this when you tell me I'm fired and kick me out?"

My eyebrows shoot up. "What? No! You're doing a great job." It's the truth. After a few days of washing dishes, he proved that he would be more useful as a bartender and bouncer. His presence has taken some of the pressure off me to constantly be tending bar. Now I can actually focus on the paperwork for the property across the street and expanding my business. "I need to step out for a bit. Tell Rafe he's in charge. I'll try to get back before last call."

His forehead creases, dark eyebrows dropping low over his green eyes. "Oh. Okay."

I can't wait around for his brain to catch up. My sweetness needs me.

Shutting myself back in my office, I close my eyes and take a few deep breaths. In my mind, I conjure up images of Penelope's building. Crumbling tan bricks. The glow of a single streetlight. Long cracks in the sidewalk. The sheen of the shitty glass entryway.

Flames heat my skin until I think I might burn to a crisp. I grit my teeth through the burn and focus on my destination. One stray thought and who knows where the fuck I'll end up. Timbuktu or the North Pole. I'd rather not find out.

A clap of thunder, then utter darkness surrounds my body.

A split second later, the distinct scent of sulfur hits my nose, and my eyes flutter open to find the very building I pictured in my head.

Teleporting isn't an exact science. Sometimes I end up a block away from where I actually wanted to go. Not to mention, the time I ended up in Phil's bathroom instead of outside his front door. Thankfully, it wasn't occupied.

But luck is on my side tonight.

I whip my phone out of my pocket and dial Penelope.

One ring later, her sweet voice fills the line. "Syn—"

"I'm outside, sweetness. Come down and let me in… *please.*" I add the last bit to hopefully disguise the franticness in my voice. Not being able to see her, touch her, it's killing me. Is she hurt?

Moments later, her feet pound on the worn cement steps as she approaches the security door. There's a red paper clutched in her hand, along with her phone. As she gets closer, and I get a better look at her, my blood simmers. Blue eyes meet mine, but they're missing their usual spark and are rimmed in red.

Mascara smudges paint the skin beneath her eyes. A few stray flakes dot the splotchy flesh of her cheeks.

Something—or *someone*—has upset my sweetness. The simmer in my veins rises to a rolling boil as my body heats.

"Hi," Penelope says as she opens the door for me.

On instinct, my hand raises to cup her face, thumb brushing over her soft but clammy cheekbone. "What happened?"

Eyes dropping to the ground, she shakes her head and, much to my dismay, steps out of my grasp. "It's been a rough day." Her sad gaze swings back to mine, a forced smile tugging at one corner of her mouth. "Come inside, and I'll explain."

"Let me get this straight..." I crumple the red paper in my hand. I've read it through about five times and still can't wrap my head around it. "You have twenty-four hours to vacate the premises?"

Penelope nods.

There's no way the building owners haven't known about the failed inspection for at least a month. I bite my tongue to hold in my growl. I've dealt with city inspectors for the apartments above the Taproom. They give you ninety days to fix any violations.

Which means, the owners of this building let that timeframe lapse, choosing to forfeit the building to the city rather than make the necessary repairs. And they made several individuals homeless in the process.

As much as it pisses me off that the owners would be so shitty, this could work in my favor.

"I have a spare room. You can move in with me."

Penelope's head snaps up, eyes widening. "What? No. That's not why I called you. I was hoping you knew of some open apartments or something."

I shrug. "And I do. Mine. You're moving in with me, sweetness. End of discussion."

"Only temporarily." She purses her lips. "Until I find a new place."

I smirk. "Sure." If that's what she needs to tell herself in order to pack her stuff and get out of this hellhole, then, yeah, *temporarily*. "What do we need to move? I'll call Xavier and have him bring his truck over."

Penelope taps a finger to her chin. "Well, the furniture was here when I moved in. So I just need to grab my clothes and toiletries. Maybe a few other things."

"Okay. That shouldn't take too long. Start packing while I call Xavier." Turning away from her, I pull up my wolven bouncer's number.

He answers after a few rings. "Yo, Syn. What's up?"

"I know it's your night off." I pinch the bridge of my nose. "But I need your help. A friend of mine needs help moving, and it's kind of... *urgent*."

"Say no more, boss. Text me the address, and I'll head over with my truck." There's a jingle of keys in the background, so he's probably already halfway out the door.

"You're a gem, Xav."

After hanging up, I shoot off a quick text with Penelope's address.

"That should be the last of it," Penelope says as she zips the jam-packed suitcase. "Guess it's a good thing I never recycled the moving boxes when I moved in last year." She smiles, but it doesn't reach her dazzling eyes.

I can't imagine coming home from work to a letter on my door telling me to get out. She must be overwhelmed.

I set the box of towels on top of the stack by the door. "How are you doing, sweetness? And don't lie to me."

"Today was... a lot. But maybe something good will come out of all of this." She waves her hand around the apartment, drawing my eyes to the chipped paint and peeling floor. I admire her optimism.

"You know, I can't say I'm disappointed that you're moving in with me." I send her a flirty grin, and her cheeks darken. "This place is a shithole."

Penelope scoffs and crosses her arms over her chest. "Yeah, but it was *my* shit hole that I paid for with *my own money* from a job that I love."

I can't help but think of the Taproom, which has come a long way from the hole in the wall it was when I opened. Now, it's a place for all walks of life to gather. A place I built for my community, with my own two hands.

Sighing, I grab her hand before I realize what I'm doing. Tingles skitter up my arm when my fingers thread through hers. A welcome feeling that has my heart picking up pace. "I get it, sweetness." My phone beeps in my other hand, breaking the moment. "Xavier's here. Let's get this show on the road so you can settle in and crash before it gets to be too late."

Between the three of us, it doesn't take long before all the boxes and bags are loaded into the back of the truck. I open the cab door so Penelope can ride in the front seat, but her eyes linger on the mouth of the alleyway next to the building.

"Oh, I need to say goodbye to Frank." Her throat muscles constrict with a swallow, and she wrings her hands in front of her. "Although, I haven't seen him in a while."

My cheeks heat, hand lifting from the truck door to scratch the shaved side of my head. "Yeah… about that."

"Syn, what aren't you telling me?"

Fuck. I spill my guts, telling her about how I offered him a job and a place to stay.

Next thing I know, her arms are wrapped around my neck, and she's squeezing the life out of me… in a good way. A stupid grin takes over my face, and I gather her in my arms, lifting her from the ground to twirl us in a circle.

"Thank you," she whispers, lips caressing the side of my neck in the softest touch that has me craving more.

More of *her*.

Chapter 9

Penelope

"Wow..." My eyes widen as I set the suitcase down and take in my new living situation. "This is really nice."

A lot nicer than where I just came from.

The walls of the bedroom are painted a moody emerald shade. Thick curtains skim the floor as Syn pulls them shut, blocking out the darkened sky and the outside world.

A large bed sits against the far wall, bracketed by two dark wood nightstands. The lamps on each are lit up, casting the room in a cozy, almost romantic, glow. Pillows of all sizes and textures rest against the modern wrought-iron headboard. All dark jewel tones that coordinate with the walls.

If *this* is the guestroom, what does her room look like?

I skim a hand over the bedspread, the material soft as silk against my palm. After the day I've had, I can't wait to dive under the covers and never surface again.

Unfortunately, the world is still turning, and things cost money. It's expensive just to exist in the city, so I have to go to work in the morning.

The silence has me turning to find Syn in the doorway, doing that sexy leaning thing that all the love interests in those smutty romance books do. Arms crossed over her chest, I get a peek of black lace through the oversized armholes of her cropped t-shirt.

With her horns swooping away from her beautiful face and the heat blooming in her eyes... Yeah, it's hot.

...And now *I'm* hot. Sweat dampens the skin on the back of my neck, and I tug the collar of my shirt. "Why would you let me stay with you?" I blurt. Apparently, this late at night, my filter disappears. *Poof!* Like Cinderella's carriage turning back into a pumpkin.

The mattress cushions my weight when my knees buckle, and I plop down. Clearing my throat, I peek up at Syn through the curtain of my stuck-together, tear-stained lashes. "That came out wrong." My shoulders shake when I heave a sigh. "What I meant was... you barely know me, why would you help me? What if I'm a bad roommate?

What if I mess up your routine? What if I'm a stalker?" The last part slips out by accident.

Syn chuckles, pushing off from the doorframe. "Sweetness, I already know you're a stalker." Hands tucked in her pockets, she swaggers over to the bed and sits next to me. Her thigh brushes against mine, setting loose a rush of butterflies in my stomach.

"I didn't mean to say that," I whisper.

Her fingers tiptoe across my leg until they reach mine, which are twisting in the hem of my cardigan. As soon as her hand engulfs mine, everything inside me settles, and I get lost in her dark gaze. "I'm kidding, but in all seriousness, do you remember what you said the night we met?"

My eyebrows dip, and I shake my head. "No."

Her shoulder bumps mine, a small smile ghosting over her mouth. "Everyone needs a little help sometimes, sweetness. Let me help you."

Tears burn my eyes, threatening to spill over. All I can do is swallow the lump in my throat and nod.

Soft lips land on my temple, and I can't help but lean into her. "Get some sleep." One last squeeze of my hand, and she heads to the door.

Before she disappears into the darkness of the hallway, Syn peers over her shoulder. Once again, the heat and longing from earlier flare to life in her eyes as she shuts the door.

Even hours later, I toss and turn in my new bed. Those lust-filled eyes have me in a chokehold. So much so that an ache blooms between my thighs, and my fingers creep beneath the waistband of my underwear.

The tip of my index finger slips easily between my folds. I'm so wet.

Bringing it higher, I bite back a moan as I circle my clit and a jolt of pleasure bows my spine.

"This is wrong," I rasp into the darkness. She's my friend. She's been kind enough to open her home to me, and here I am, masturbating to thoughts of her.

Ripping my hand away from my core, I flop onto my side, punching my pillow a few times to get comfortable.

What would Mom say if she knew what I'd just done?

She'd say there's something wrong with me. That I'm not trying hard enough to find a man.

I don't want a man...

I want Syn.

But I can't have her.

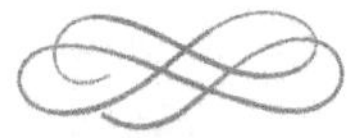

It's official: I'm avoiding my roommate. It's been almost a week of living with Syn, and besides a pleasant "Hello" or "Goodbye," we've been like two ships passing in the night.

I get up early to catch the subway to work, and she's still sleeping. When I get home in the evenings, she's already gone to the Taproom for the night. And I do not have the guts to go down and socialize, even though it's literally right downstairs.

I take a sip of my white chocolate mocha, closing my eyes to savor the rich cocoa as it slides down my throat. If I'm ensnared by her starless, heated gaze one more time, I might do something I'll regret.

"Hey, good job closing your first sale yesterday," Annie says, clinking her mug against mine. The lavender from her tea tickles my nostrils as she pulls back to take a sip.

At least one thing is going right. My career is finally falling into place. "Thanks." I smile, cheeks burning. "I didn't know there would be such a confidence boost from it."

"You know what you're doing, Pen. Don't let your nerves, or that asshole from last week, stifle your flame."

"I won't."

White flashes in my periphery before Vanessa plops into the booth next to Annie. "I'm so sorry I'm late. A certain minotaur was very grumpy when I told him I was leaving for brunch, but I need some girl time. It's been too long," she says, pushing her long, wavy hair over her shoulder. Something on her left ring finger glitters as she rests her hands on the table.

I gasp, grabbing her hand. "When did this happen?"

"And you didn't tell us?" Annie glares at our vampire friend, although the gesture is playful.

Vanessa's fangs peek out when she smiles. "We went to a cute B&B in Vermont a few weeks ago, and Luc popped the question. I wanted to tell you both in person, but things have been crazy busy juggling Urban Oasis and Hidden Oasis."

After meeting her mate, Luc, Vanessa ended up opening a second spa location in a small town outside the city so they could be together full time. They did long distance for a while, but she was miserable.

"I'm so happy for you!" I squeeze her hand.

Annie wraps her in a hug. "Congratulations, Ness."

"Thank you. And you know you'll both be invited to the wedding. Luc suggested eloping, but I think my mom would disown me if I didn't let her help me plan everything." She laughs as the waitress comes to take our orders.

As Vanessa and Annie chat, I nod along, but my mind somehow strays back to Syn. She exudes confidence, something I envy, being a wallflower my whole life. She's so sure of everything she does, from buying a new property to all but demanding I stay with her.

And don't get me started on how she radiates this rough and powerful sexual aura. Once again, that's something I've never had experience with. I've never felt sexy or confident in my skin.

Is that why I'm enamored by her? She's the complete opposite of me, yet I crave even an ounce of time in her presence.

"Have either of you ever been with a woman?" The question is out of my mouth before I know what's happening.

Vanessa chokes, covering her mouth as she gulps down her coffee.

Annie reaches over and pats Vanessa's back until she stops coughing.

My eyes drop to the table as warmth fills my cheeks. "Sorry. That was too personal. I shouldn't have asked. Forget I said anything." My fingers fiddle with the napkin under my mug.

A soft hand cups mine, stopping my fidgeting. "Pen, look at me. Please." Annie's steady voice has my gaze lifting. She flashes me a kind smile. "We're friends, right?"

I nod.

"Nothing's too personal between us."

Vanessa adds her hand to the pile. "Same. I'm sure you've figured out by now that I have no filter. And, yes, I have been with women and men. Human. Monster. Together. Separate. You name it, I've probably done it." She winks, which has the flush on my cheeks spreading down my neck. "Why do you ask?"

"Umm. Well, I met this woman a few weeks ago, and I can't stop thinking about her."

"Have you told her this?" Annie asks. She knows that I'm living with Syn now, so it wouldn't be hard for her to put two and two together.

I shake my head, gripping the warm sides of my mug when they pull their hands away. "She's my friend. I shouldn't be having these kinds of feelings about her."

"Why not?" Vanessa asks.

Shrugging, I run my nail over the spaceship logo on my mug. "I don't know." My phone buzzes in my pocket, and I slip it out to find a text from my mom.

Mom: I'm in the city visiting a friend for the weekend. Lunch tomorrow at Le Champ D'or. Noon. Don't be late and dress appropriately.

The message has my gut sinking. Mom would probably have an aneurism if she knew I was questioning my sexuality. I gulp and shove the phone back into my jeans before looking back at Vanessa and Annie. "Forget I said anything, okay?"

Annie's black eyebrows pinch. "Oh... sure." She pats my hand again. "But if you need to talk, we're here for you."

"Day or night," Vanessa adds.

I nod, swallowing down the bile in my throat.

No matter how much I want Syn, she isn't meant for me.

Chapter 10

Penelope

"Do I look okay?" I skim my hands down my thighs, smoothing the faux leather fabric into place. Peeking over my shoulder, I find Syn with her back braced against my doorframe.

Flashbacks of the night I moved in bombard me as she crosses one leg over the other and smirks. "*Damn*, sweetness. You look hot."

The sultry rasp of her voice combined with the compliment has a furious blush coating my cheeks and chest. "Thank you," I say, eyes skimming my reflection in the decorative mirror leaned against my bedroom wall. "I splurged after I got my bonus from my first sale last week.

Are you sure it's not too garish?" The black snakeskin material glides through my fingers as they play with the hem. I was hoping it would act as armor, giving me the strength to fend off Mom's judgmental stares.

But I'm afraid the sleek fabric is a false bravado.

Pushing off the door, she comes to stand behind me and rests her hands on my shoulders. "Absolutely not. It suits you." Her energy swirls around me, and I roll my shoulders back. "I thought we could hang out after you get home from lunch with the wicked witch."

"Syn!" I spin to face her, hands fisted on my hips.

With a devilish smirk pulling at one corner of her lips, Syn raises her hands in surrender. "Sorry, but if it walks like a duck and quacks like a duck… I'll be waiting with ice cream and two spoons when you get home," she says before winking and heading toward the door.

After a final glance in the mirror, I grab my shoes and follow her into the living room.

On the couch, a strip of sunlight spilling through the window bathes Fenrir in a golden glow. His lush black fur calls to my fingers. Shiny and soft.

I give in, diving them into the thick strands along his back. Oblivious to the ocean waves crashing in my stomach, he groans and stretches. "It'll be fine." It has to be. "I'm sure she just wants to confirm my plans for Labor Day weekend."

Syn scoffs. "Just don't let her set you up on another date. Okay, sweetness? Don't let her bully you."

"I won't." With great reluctance, I slip my fingers from Fen's fur. As much as I wish I could stay here, in the safety of Syn's apartment, I can't. If I avoid Mom, it'll make things worse. I stuff my feet into my shoes and grab my purse on my way to the door. "But I won't say no to ice cream... since you're offering."

"Oh, I'm offering, sweetness." Her sinful laughter follows me into the hallway as I shut the door.

I don't know what the heck I'm doing. The subtle touches, flirty banter, and downright molten stares make it abundantly clear Syn is attracted to me, but I'm the one standing in my own way. Why?

Why can't I get over my mother's expectations and dive headfirst into whatever Syn and I could have?

It could end in heartbreak.

Or it could be the best decision I've ever made.

I wish I could take the leap... but right now, I can't.

"Penelope? What are you doing here?" A familiar deep voice has my head snapping up to a large man ascending the stairs.

"Do I know you?" I sneak a hand into my purse, fingers searching for the pepper spray I keep nestled in the side pocket.

A slow, easy grin spreads across his face, wrinkling the corners of his eyes. "It's me... Frank."

My eyebrows skyrocket to my hairline. "Frank?" The man before me—with his brown hair tied in a bun and dark, neatly trimmed stubble lining his jaw—does not resemble the Frank I last saw almost a month ago.

I take a step closer, squinting as I scan his sweat-soaked t-shirt and jogging shorts. When my eyes finally land on his face, his emerald gaze holds the same warmth as my friend. "What are you doing here?" Once the question leaves my lips, I remember Syn explaining how she offered him a place to stay and a job.

"Syn's helping me out. What about you? You're living with her now?" The smirk that follows could melt butter.

"Oh, ummm... yeah. The city condemned our old building—"

"'Bout fucking time." He crosses his arms over his chest. "She's one of the good ones, you know?"

I nod.

His eyes radiate sincerity as he speaks the next part. "Hang onto her."

Does he think...? "Oh, we're not together."

Wrestling his keys from his pocket, Frank flashes another smirk my way. "Sure." Then he slips into the apartment across the hall.

We're not. *Right?*

Although, Syn's small gestures would prove otherwise. There's always a pot of coffee waiting when I wake up in the morning with a note next to it.

On Monday, I almost burst into tears when I saw

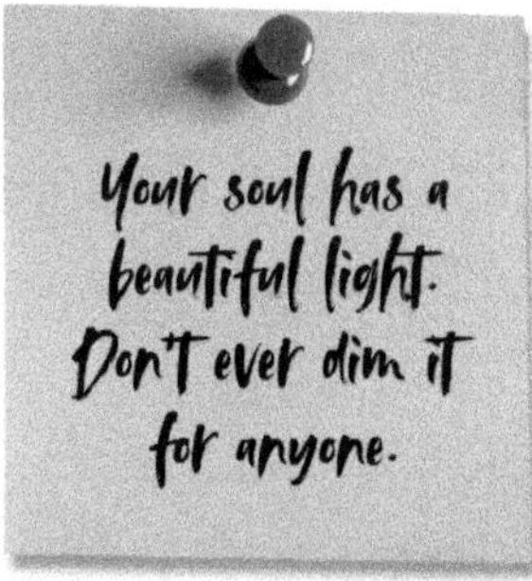

written in her messy handwriting.

It was the same thing on Wednesday.

And Friday.

Like she has a window into my soul. Like she really sees me.

Each little purple sticky note drives her deeper into my heart. And I'm afraid we're dangerously close to blowing right past the friendzone and into something bigger and brighter.

Plus, it seems I'm not fooling anyone—myself, included—that Syn and I aren't heading down a path that ends with one of us in the other's bed.

My phone dings in my purse, breaking my thought spiral. I pull it out to find a text from my mom.

Mom: Don't be late, Penelope.

Dread coils in my stomach as I trudge down the stairs, feet heavy as bricks, and hail a cab to take me across town. I have to tell Mom no more dates. Maybe then I'll have the courage to pursue Syn.

Ugh. Time to face the music.

The ostentatious gold doors of Le Champ D'Or loom before me. Mom would pick a stuffy, upscale restaurant for our lunch.

What I wouldn't give for a greasy cheeseburger and some fries right now. In agreement, my stomach grumbles, reminding me that I forgot to eat breakfast this morning. My poor tummy has been in knots for days now... since moving in with Syn, when my world turned upside down.

Soft classical music surrounds me as I approach the maître d' stand. The suit-clad man behind the desk smiles and says, "Good afternoon. Will you be dining alone today?"

"No. Actually, I'm meeting someone. Caryn Martin."

Finger scanning the seating chart, he nods. "Right this way."

As we approach the table, frigid blue eyes scan me from head to toe. My mom's lips purse when her gaze lingers on my skirt. So much for my armor. I tug at the hem with clammy fingers.

"Finally," Mom snaps as I slip into my seat across from her. "Didn't I teach you the value of punctuality, Penelope?"

My cheeks warm, and my eyes slide to the waiter, who winces. *Lunch with a side of public humiliation, anyone? A Caryn Martin specialty.* "Mom, it's only two after—"

"No matter." She brushes me off and turns her attention to the waiter. "Now that my daughter has graced us with her presence, we'd like to order." Mom rattles off her order while I scan the menu, pointing to a random dish I recognize.

Once he's gone, the full weight of her piercing gaze lands on me.

It takes everything in me not to hunch forward and wrap my arms around my middle. I'm almost thirty, for crying out loud. I should be able to stand up to my own mother and take control of my life.

Silence lingers between us, nearly choking all the oxygen from the air. She's extra icy today.

"H-How's Dad?" I force a smile onto my face, but it's brittle and tight.

"Your father is in California for a case." Being a high-power defense attorney, he was gone a lot when I was younger. Thus, he was blind to the harsh treatment from the woman across the table from me. And when Colin left for college, my buffer was completely gone.

"Oh."

"But I think we need to address the elephant in the room. Don't you, Penelope?"

Fingers taking on a life of their own, they fiddle with the stark-white tablecloth that hangs over my legs. "What elephant?"

Mom waves a hand at me. "How will you attract a successful man if you're dressed like a harlot?"

I knew she'd hate this skirt and, subconsciously, maybe that's why I bought it. A silent act of rebellion after being the perfect doll for too long.

Mouth agape, I glance down at the simple black tank top I paired with the faux-leather skirt. It's tasteful and sophisticated, if you ask me. Modest even, only a hint of cleavage peeking over the neckline. "Harlot?" I mumble, but she's moved on to bigger and better fish.

"And don't think I don't know what you did to poor Matthew," she seethes, teeth bared.

Harsh laughter spills from my mouth before I can stop it. "Matthew. You mean the misogynistic jerk? Don't you even care that I was evicted from my apartment a few days ago?"

Mom gasps, clutching the pearl necklace around her neck. "Evicted? What did you do? Where are you living? Not with that dreadful dragon."

Of course, being evicted would somehow be *my* fault. "No. A friend is letting me stay with her until I find a new place."

"And what is her name? What does she do for a living?"

"Her name is Synthea. She owns the Synful Taproom over on 7th and Crawford."

"A bar?" Her voice rises to an ear-piercing octave. "I bet she's a real winner."

"Mom! She—"

"You've fallen so far since you left home. Assaulting Matthew, dressing like... like *this*." She waves a hand at my perfectly acceptable outfit. "Now living with some low-life drug dealer."

Whoa. How did we jump from bar owner to drug dealer?

"Mom—"

"I'm disappointed, Penelope. No matter." She smiles at me. "We can fix this."

"I don't want to fix—"

Condescension oozing from her perfectly concealed pores—heaven forbid anyone know her real age—she pats the back of my hand. "Luckily, Camilla's son is newly single.

I pull my hand out from under hers. "Mom—"

Once again, she steamrolls over me, like I'm not even at the darn table. "He's forty, so a little older than you, but that's fine. It just means you'll be giving me a grandchild soon." The glee that fills her voice at the mention of grandkids has me swallowing the urge to vomit.

After being cut off not once, but *three* times, I've had it. "Enough!" Plates and silverware rattle when I slam my palms onto the table, shaking the whole thing. "You're not listening to me. No more dates... *please*."

Mom gasps at my outburst, clutching those stupid pearls again. I wish I could rip them off her neck and stomp on them. "There's no need to cause a scene, Penelope. He's available next Tuesday—"

Taking my cue from the master of interruption, I cut her off again. "Stop, Mom. I'm done." My head pounds, but I keep going. I'm on a roll. I can't stop now. "Stop with the dates. Stop with the baby stuff. I don't even know if I want kids."

"Don't be ridiculous, Penelope. Every woman wants to be a mother."

Yeah, some mother you were. Leaving me with Colin or a babysitter so you could spend your days at the country club.

"No. They don't, Mom. You're living in the dark ages. Women have choices. We can prioritize our careers over having babies."

Mom's perfectly made-up face crumples into an ugly scowl. "Is that dragon woman filling your head with these obtuse thoughts?"

"Don't blame Antoinette... She supports me more than you ever have. I-I'm done." Similar to the night I threw water on Matthew, some inner strength I never knew I had takes over, filling my body as I roll my shoulders back and stand. The napkin clutched in my sweaty palm lands on the table. "Goodbye, Mom."

In that moment, I don't know if I mean goodbye forever or just for today. All I know is I *have* to get out of here.

"Penelope! Get back here this instant!" Mom's voice is muffled over the blood pounding in my ears. I've never stood up to her like this. My fingers are numb at my sides, and a cold sweat slicks the back of my neck.

Body moving on autopilot, I barrel out of the restaurant and onto the crowded New York City sidewalk. Lightning strikes my temples with every step I take, and my lungs can't get enough oxygen, making me dizzy.

Somehow, even in the haze of an adrenaline induced panic attack, I manage to hail a cab and get home.

The herd of elephants dancing in my head has me squinting as I open the door and tumble into the apartment.

From her seat at the kitchen table, Syn's head snaps up, nail polish brush held midair. "Whoa. You okay, sweetness?"

I collapse into the chair across from her. "Not exactly." A particularly harsh jolt of pain strikes behind my eye, and I wince. Bringing a hand to my face, I rub the socket until the wave of pain dissipates.

"Wanna talk about it?" Syn swipes black polish over her middle fingernail, which is noticeably shorter than the rest. Same with her ring fingernail.

I shake my head, which sends another nausea inducing spark through my brain. "Why are those nails shorter?" I ask in hopes of distracting myself from the impending migraine.

"All the better to finger you with, sweetness," she purrs, then flashes me a wicked smirk that would have my insides liquifying if I wasn't struggling to stay upright.

Instead, I splutter, unsure how to respond to the blatant sexual advance.

Syn chuckles, the sound rich and warm, soothing some of the ache in my head. "I'm kidding, Pen. You should see your face. How did lunch go?"

"Not great. I don't feel very good. I'm going to go lay down."

Her playfulness melts into concern. "Oh, okay. I was going to make some pasta for dinner. Want me to wake you when it's ready?"

I nod before heading to my room.

Drawing the thick velvet curtains closed, the room is bathed in darkness. My skirt drops to the floor with a *plop* as I wiggle out of it and slip into a pair of soft cotton shorts.

I scrounge through my purse in search of my medication, but come up empty-handed. I'm not sure where it ended up in my hasty move and haven't needed it since that night. *Great.* Static fills the center of my vision, and a fiery wave of numbness spreads from my fingertips up my arm. It's too late to fight off this attack anyway. The only thing that will help is sleep.

Crawling under the covers, the last thing I see is a text from my mom.

> **Mom: Well, your little tantrum worked. Are you happy now, Penelope? No more dates... if you bring someone to Labor Day dinner in a few weeks.**

It's a small victory, but it's a start.

Chapter 11

Synthea

I toss another handful of spinach into the pot, using my wooden spoon to fold it into the sauce-covered pasta. A comforting aroma wafts off the noodles, and I breathe deeply. “Mmm. Hopefully, this makes Penelope feel better.” I glance over my shoulder at the dark hallway that leads to the bedrooms and bathroom. It’s been quiet since she went to her room a few hours ago.

Once the spinach is wilted in, I place the lid on and switch off the burner. Fenrir has taken up his usual spot on the sofa. His feet twitch before a low, ragged snore leaves his snout. “Some guard you are,” I say, passing behind the couch and making my way down the hall to Penelope's bedroom.

My knuckles rap against the wooden door. No response.

"Sweetness," I call in a soft voice before knocking again.

Still nothing.

I wrap my hand around the knob and push the door open a few inches. Just enough for a sliver of fading daylight to drift down the hall and illuminate the lump under the blankets.

"Pen? Are you awake?" My words are met by silence, which has me crossing the distance between us on quiet feet.

In her sleep, Penelope's brow is creased, and her face is scrunched. I run a hand over her forehead, the need to touch her too strong to ignore. Her skin is a little warm, but nothing concerning. "Hey, you've been sleeping for a while. Why don't you come and eat something? I made pasta." The sweet, herby aroma of the pasta sauce wafts into the bedroom.

The answering groan that leaves Penelope's lips has every hair on my body prickling. Something's wrong.

"Sweetness." I stroke my hand over her hair. "When did you eat last?"

"Forgot breakfast," she rasps. "Too busy fighting with Mom at lunch..."

Alarm bells sound in my brain. "So you haven't eaten anything today?"

Penelope groans again as a shaky hand raises to rub her temple. "Migraine. Need sleep."

"You need to eat, baby girl. I'll be right back."

Back in the kitchen, I scarf down a bowlful of pasta in as few bites as possible before filling another one for Penelope. Along with a glass of water, I bring everything back to the bedroom with me.

When I turn on the bedside lamp, Penelope whines and burrows under the covers. I'm not super familiar with migraines, but from the little I do know, light sensitivity and excruciating pain are top of the list. "I know it hurts, sweetness. Take a few bites for me, please." Loading the fork with a few penne noodles and a bite of sausage, I wait for my caterpillar to emerge from her cocoon.

Like a good girl, Penelope takes a bite. Eyes closed, she moans as I slide the tines of the fork from her lips, and it takes everything in me not to tackle her to the bed and have my way with her.

She's in pain, Syn. Not the time.

Thank fuck, I had the foresight to pop a straw into the glass of water, otherwise I don't know how I'd get her to drink any.

It's even one of those silly, brightly colored corkscrew ones. Sue me for adding a little fun into my life.

I smile as Pen wraps her lips around the neon yellow plastic and takes a few gulps, which warms my insides. Do these migraines happen often? Is it because she hasn't eaten all day? She needs to take better care of herself. Until she does, I'll do it for her.

Once I'm satisfied that her belly is full, I gather the bowl and glass. Penelope's hand shoots out from under the blanket, fingers clutching my arm. "Stay." Her voice is soft, but there's no mistaking the request.

"I'll be right back. Gotta clean up the kitchen." At my words, her hand falls away, and she nuzzles back into her blanket nest.

Like a demon in the night—literally—I tiptoe out of the room and shut the door behind me, but leave it cracked in case my sweetness calls out for me.

"Where's my cupcake?" the gruff voice asks in my head as glowing red eyes appear in the darkness.

Fenrir follows me into the kitchen. "Penelope doesn't feel good. She's resting," I say, shooting him a glance over my shoulder while I scoop the leftover pasta into containers.

His furry brow scrunches. *"Did you try cuddles? According to the box with the moving pictures, cuddles solve many problems."*

Setting the dirty pot in the sink, I fill it with hot water and a squirt of dish soap. I bite my cheek to stifle a laugh. "You watch too much TV, Fen."

The click of his toenails against the tile floor is the only response I get when he turns tail and leaves the room.

Once the mess from dinner is cleaned up, I make a pit stop to the bathroom. I have a feeling I'll be spending the night in Penelope's room… Not something I mind a single bit, but my bladder might.

Even demons need to pee.

After washing my hands, I grab a bottle of pain relievers from the medicine cabinet before heading back to the bedroom.

The blanket rises and falls with Penelope's steady breathing, a soft snore spilling from her parted lips when I slip under the covers next to her.

I wrap my arm around her middle, but my hand is met by thick fur. "You're just a big softie, aren't you?"

Fenrir raises his head, one luminous eye opening a sliver. "*No. You didn't see anything. This is purely for the cupcake's sake. Nothing more.*" Using his giant paw, he tucks Penelope's petite form against his warm body.

Liar. "Mhmm." Resting my hand on top of his paw, I close my eyes and breathe in Penelope's sweet vanilla scent.

She whimpers in her sleep, tucking her head to the side of my neck. "Don't leave."

"Never, sweetness." Like a magnet, my hand is drawn to her, smoothing over the golden strands of hair that are tied into a messy bun. On their return path, my fingers find her temple, rubbing circles into the skin.

I've healed myself before. A paper cut here, a sprained ankle there, but I've never tried my powers on anyone else. Let alone a migraine. My lids fall closed, and I inhale deep, focusing all my attention on my fingers. Frenetic electricity rushes down my arm and into my fingertips.

When my lids flutter open, we're cast in a soft purple glow emitted from the tips of my fingers.

"Mmm. That feels good," Penelope moans, leaning into my touch.

It must be working, so I continue rubbing slow circles on her temple until Penelope's breathing evens out and my lids grow heavy. With my sweetness cocooned between me and Fen, I drift into what's sure to be the best sleep of my centuries-long life.

Chapter 12

My nose brushes against something warm and... *fluffy*? Slowly, to not upset the hippos doing gymnastics in my head, I peel one eyelid open. Midnight fur fills my visual field, causing my other eye to follow suit, springing wide.

Head braced on the pillow next to mine, Fenrir's massive jaw hangs open, tongue draped over his vicious teeth. His chest expands, and a rough snore rumbles from his muzzle. I bite my cheek and slap a hand over my mouth to stop my laughter.

Who knew hellhounds were such big teddy bears?

A heavy weight around my waist has my eyes trekking south to find his giant paw curled over me. Even in sleep, he's protecting me.

There's a noticeable emptiness at my back. I peek over my shoulder to find the sheets rumpled, but no purple-haired demon.

As much as my heart deflates, it's probably for the best. Memories of yesterday are a little hazy, but I do remember the text from Mom before I crashed. Just because she agreed to let me find my own date for Labor Day doesn't mean she'd suddenly be on board if I showed up with a woman, let alone a non-human one.

One of the hippos chooses that moment to slam into my temple. I crush my eyes shut and snuggle into Fen's lush fur with a groan. First order of business this morning: find my migraine meds. Fen lets out another snore, his paw tightening around me. A little more sleep wouldn't hurt either.

"You two look cozy." The humor-filled, sultry voice has me scrambling to sit up. In the doorway, Syn chuckles before taking a sip from her mug.

Behind me, Fenrir is completely unperturbed by my sudden movement and the dip in the mattress when Syn rests her weight on the edge. "Morning, sweetness." Her eyes scan from my messy hair down to the thin tank top I threw on yesterday.

Giving away my state of confused arousal, my traitorous nipples harden behind the fabric. "Oh, um, hi," I squeak before dragging the comforter up to cover my flushed chest. "I'm sorry about yesterday. I didn't mean to ruin your evening or be a burden—"

A finger lands on my lips, shutting me up. "Let's get one thing straight, Penelope. You're not a burden. Not with me. Ever. But I would like to know what happened yesterday and how I can help in the future."

My eyes double in size. "Oh. You would?"

Syn nods. "Yes. So if you're feeling up to it, I have some breakfast coming from Cream Me Up. Would you care to join me?"

"Yes. Oh, crap! What time is it? I need to text Antoinette and tell her I won't be in today."

She pats my leg over the blankets, but the faint warmth from her touch has me nearly melting into a puddle. "Take your time. I'll be waiting on the couch." Then she leaves me alone with my muddled mess of thoughts.

I fumble for my phone where it lays on the nightstand. After sending a quick text to Annie, I flip the blankets back and get up.

The room spins, my legs wobble, and my brain feels like it's going to implode. "Whoa." Clutching my head in one hand, I plop back onto the bed.

Where did I put those stupid meds? I can't get caught off guard like this again.

Neon yellow in my periphery catches my attention. A full glass of water with a bright yellow crazy straw and a bottle of pain relievers wait on the nightstand. "Oh, thank goodness." Muscles weak and hungover from the attack, I finally get the childproof lid open and shake two red pills into my palm. I toss them into my mouth and suck down almost the whole cup of water.

For most of my adult life, I've kept my migraines to myself since I didn't want to be a burden or thought less of. Annie knows because, well, she's my boss. She covered for me a time or two when we worked for our old boss.

Syn knows now. She knows that behind the perfect facade, there are cracks.

She said you're not a burden, though. Remember? She wants to take care of you.

Yeah, for how long?

A foot, or rather, a paw to my back has the self-deprecation flitting from my mind. Fast asleep, Fenrir has officially spread his big body and taken over the entirety of my bed. "Guess that's my cue to get up," I say, poking his toe. Reflexively, it curls, but the hellhound doesn't wake.

Once I've left the warmth of my bed, a chill trembles my body, reminding me of the exposed state of my nipples. I can't very well face Syn, my supposed friend, with laser beams shooting from my chest. *Hey! Look at me!* my boobs might as well be screaming.

"This isn't awkward at all." Shuffling on heavy feet to the closet, I find the box with my winter clothes inside. At least, I think that's what's in here. In all honesty, I packed in such a haze, I'm not sure if the boxes are labeled correctly.

Thumbnail slicing the tape, I rip the box open. Right on top of a neatly folded stack of sweatshirts... my migraine medication. "That's where you've been hiding." The purple and turquoise box taunts me as I snatch it up and place it on the nightstand.

Then I chuck on a well-loved, worn hoodie that falls past the hem of my sleep shorts before leaving Fen to his nap.

True to her word, Syn is waiting on the couch when I enter the living room. Attention focused on the coffee table, she's busy taking containers out of a pink paper bag, so I spend a few seconds admiring the sharp slope of her nose and the sleek angles of her cheekbones as the morning sun streaks across her face. Dark-gray lips split into a smug grin before black eyes snap to me. My breath stalls in my lungs.

"Staring again, sweetness?"

"Who? Me?" I tuck my hands into the pouch on my hoodie and round the couch. "I would never," I say while I plop down next to her.

"Mhmm." Her eyes twinkle with mirth as they slide from me to the spread of takeout containers on the table. Using a single finger, Syn flips the lid to reveal a sight that has my stomach grumbling. "I didn't know what you liked, so I had Phil drop off a little bit of everything."

The scent of greasy, salty goodness hits my nose as she slides the container in front of me. It's the perfect mix of everything Cream Me Up is known for. Nestled on a bed of perfectly crisp hash browns is a pile of fluffy, cheesy eggs and a few slices of perfectly cooked bacon.

Syn opens another container. Sugary glaze melts over the top of a smaller version of their signature ooey-gooey cinnamon roll.

"This looks amazing," I say, grabbing a fork from the table. "I get really hungry after an attack, so this is perfect."

Syn's nails click against her phone screen while she types something. "Good. I'll write that down for next time. What else should I know?" Her gaze swings up to meet mine.

"It's fine." I take a bite of bacon and nearly moan when it melts on my tongue. "I found my meds. I'll be okay next time."

"Penelope." Her voice is stern. *Uh-oh.* "As long as you live here, I want to take care of you."

My eyes burn, dipping to my lap as I swallow another bite. Besides Jenn and Colin, no one has helped me navigate the ups and downs of my chronic illness. I've dealt with the impending anxiety of waiting for the next attack, the inevitable depression because it feels like my body is failing me… All of it, I've managed on my own for so long, never wanting to burden someone else. "Why?" I peer up at her through the shield of my lashes.

A single, clipped laugh bursts from her mouth. "In case it wasn't abundantly clear, I like you. A lot."

I cough as a mouthful of bacon goes down wrong. "As a friend, right?"

Not breaking eye contact, she declares, "For now."

The sureness in her answer has me gulping a harsh swallow. She has no intention of letting me slip behind my mask and brush her off. *Suck it up, buttercup. Pull those big girl panties on and let someone in...for real this time.*

No more masking.

No more hiding.

Cracks and all, put it out there.

"Okay. Let's start from the beginning..."

While we eat, I give Syn the abridged version of when the migraine attacks started in my late teens and how my mom was less than supportive. Anger vibrates her body with each word that tumbles from my mouth.

"And these meds... they help?"

"In a way. The abortive meds, when taken in time, can reduce the severity of the aura—"

"The aura? That's the sensory stuff?"

"Right. The zigzags in my vision. Not being able to come up with certain words. Numbness on one side of my body. They're all warning signs that a migraine is coming. The medication shortens the aura duration and, usually, makes the impending headache more bearable. But I couldn't find them yesterday, so I had to suffer through."

The whole time I talk, Syn diligently takes notes on her phone, not missing a single detail. "Did you find your meds? Do we need to get more?"

We, not you. Something about the willingness to take on part of the responsibility has me ready to burst into tears. "I found them."

She nods. "Good. What triggered the attack yesterday?"

Now that we've finished eating, I've tucked myself under a fuzzy blanket. My fingers toy with the edge, eyes refusing to meet Syn's. "It's hard to say. My triggers aren't exactly the same every time. Dehydration, low blood sugar, hormonal changes, stress, lack of sleep... they all play a part, so it's hard to predict when an attack is coming. Sometimes, I have multiple attacks a month. Other times, I'll go six months without anything."

"I'm so sorry, Penelope. That sounds overwhelming."

You have no idea. I blow out a breath, the dam holding tears back, ready to crack at any minute. "It's exhausting. I try to manage everything the best I can, without letting the anxiety of a possible migraine keep me from living my life."

Her hand landing on mine stops my fidgeting. "Penelope, I'm here to help, okay? Please, let me."

I gulp. "I'll try."

"That's all I ask. So what happened yesterday?"

"Well, not eating all day probably didn't help..."

Syn rolls her eyes.

"And telling my mom off probably didn't either," I whisper, face collapsing into a wince.

"You told her to get fucked?" There's a level of joy in her voice that I try to ignore.

My head pops up. "Syn!"

"What? She had it coming." Setting her phone on the table, she gives me every morsel of her attention. "I'm proud of you for finding your voice." The space between us dissipates as I get lost in her dark gaze. "You're powerful, Penelope Martin; you just don't believe it yet." She reaches out, tucking a stray lock of hair behind my ear, and I can't stop the shiver that courses through me. "And until you do, I'll believe in you enough for the both of us."

Helpless to the longing swirling around us, I lean closer, until my breath mingles with hers. "I think I like having you in my corner."

Her fingers ghost along my jaw, eyes dipping to my parted lips. "I think I like being in your corner, sweetness."

"Well, isn't this just precious? My baby sister and a human, all cuddled up." The foreign voice has me springing back from Syn until I'm plastered to the arm of the couch.

When I look back, a raven-haired woman with skin and horns that match Syn's stands behind us, with a blistering glare aimed right at *me*.

Chapter 13

Synthea

"Lucie," I growl, low and deep, as sulfur permeates my senses. "What the fuck are you doing here?"

"Can't I check on my baby sister? I did raise you, after all." Using a single finger, she nudges the empty to-go containers aside before sitting on the edge of the coffee table and crossing one stiletto-clad foot over the other.

When her eyes land on Penelope, I puff out my arms and angle my body to block her view. A possessive warning rumbles from my chest.

"Am I interrupting something?" she asks, playing innocent.

"You know you are," I counter.

"Who's your friend?" She leans to the right, no doubt trying to get a better view, but I anticipate her movement, moving my body to shield Penelope.

Except, my sweetness isn't having it. An elbow presses into my side before she wiggles out from behind me and extends her hand toward my sister. "I'm Penelope." Her dimpled smile would disarm anyone. *Damn, she's beautiful.* Even in her current disheveled, sleep-rumpled state. "Who are you?"

As predicted, Lucie's upper lip peels back to expose her sharp teeth, and she glares at Penelope's hand, like it's personally offended her. "I, little girl, am the *Queen* of Hell. Piss me off, and I'll crush you like that." She snaps her crimson claws an inch from Penelope, whose eyes widen and her mouth drops open.

Me, on the other hand, my body vibrates, resisting the urge to break Lucie's fingers for being so close to what's mine. Before I can do any such thing, my sister's dark gaze slices to me. "Of course you'd fall for a *human*. You're just like him."

The insult lands like a dagger through my heart, intentionally searing.

"This again? So what if I am?" I stand and spread my arms wide. "My mother was the best thing to happen to Dad. He told me himself."

Mirroring me, Lucie stands, meeting my heaving chest with hers. "You're wrong. He was a fool! I told you before, we're not meant to love. It clouded his judgment. Left him weak and exposed. She's the reason he's dead!"

My harsh breathing nearly muffles the gasp Penelope sucks in.

"You need to leave. Before you say something else you'll regret." I point to the door, even though she won't use it.

"I hope she's worth it," Lucie spits. But her voice softens when she says, "I wouldn't wish his fate onto you, Sister. Be careful."

"I know what I'm doing." *Do I?* The slight wobble in my voice leaves the cracks in my armor on display.

With a final lingering glance between me and Penelope, Lucie dips her head before she disappears in a burst of flames.

Once she's gone, I drop onto the couch. Elbows resting on my knees, I hang my head.

"So... you have a sister... and she's the Queen of Hell. Wasn't expecting that." Penelope's voice is a mere whisper.

My humorless laugh adds to the tension filling the room. "Forgot to mention that."

"She seems... *nice*?"

Head swinging up, I look over my shoulder at Penelope. Bottom lip trapped under her teeth, she twists her hands in her lap.

"Really?" I raise a single eyebrow.

When she smiles, her dimples pop, soothing the beast Lucie awoke. "No. She seems like she hates me."

I sigh. "She doesn't hate *you*, per se. She hates what you represent. What all humans represent."

"Which is?"

"Weakness. Distraction."

"Because a human was responsible for your dad's death?"

"That's how she sees it." Messy purple strands tangle on my nails when I sift a hand through the back of my hair.

"And how do you see it?" Penelope arches an expectant blonde eyebrow at me.

I can't help but smile. "Are you sure you want to know my damage?"

Her grin widens. "I'll show you mine if you show me yours." And when she winks—yeah, all the oxygen leaves my lungs.

How can I say no to this precious creature?

Naïve to the inner workings of Hell and the centuries I spent alongside the literal Devil. Do I really want to sully her with my past?

"Come on, Syn." She bumps my shoulder with hers. "I promise, I won't judge."

I have no doubt.

Blowing out a breath, I spin to face her, tucking one knee against the back of the couch. "Where should I start?"

Warm fingers curl around mine where my hand rests in my lap. "The beginning seems like a pretty good place."

With my focus narrowed on her bright blue eyes, I do as she says. "My dad is—*was*—the King of Hell. The Devil. Lucifer. Whatever you want to call it."

No surprise, Penelope's eyes grow comically wide. "So the Devil, Hell… it's all real?"

I nod. "I mean, dragons and vampires are real… Does this part really surprise you?"

She rolls her eyes, and I fucking love the little hint of attitude from my good girl. "Okay. Point made. Keep going."

My throat constricts around the lump lodged there, and I force it down. "Centuries ago, he came to the surface."

"Is that normal? For the Devil to leave Hell?"

"Not usually. Under normal circumstances, only lesser demons conduct business in this world. But these weren't normal circumstances. A young woman summoned a demon, and he was called to answer her by some mysterious force."

Her eyebrows scrunch. "Like fate."

I'd imagine it's the same tug that drew me to Penelope the night she walked into my bar. I shrug. "Sure. We'll call it fate. She was dying and wanted to make a bargain."

"Your mom?" Pen whispers.

Smiling, I nod. "Dad was struck by her beauty. I suppose you'd say it was a case of instant love." I chuckle. "He healed her on the spot and didn't even ask for her soul in return. At the disapproval of his advisors, he continued to visit her, and their attraction blossomed into something real. Something that transcended time and space. The Devil falling in love with a human? It was impossible." My voice drops to a whisper. "At least, it should have been."

When I glance up at Penelope, her eyes are glossy with unshed tears. Fingers still laced through mine, I bring our joined hands to my mouth and press my lips to her knuckles.

"Then what happened?"

"She got pregnant... I think you know how that happens." My saucy wink has a rosy hue painting her cheeks. That innocent blush has quickly become one of my favorite things. "She died... giving birth to me. Unfortunately, even the Devil can't resurrect someone from the dead. He couldn't save her a second time."

The space between us disappears. Along with her slender arms, Penelope's vanilla scent wraps me in a soothing embrace. "Syn, I'm so sorry."

I shrug. "I survived. Dad brought me to Hell, but his heart was shattered. He was a shell of his former self, or at least that's what Lucie says. She raised me, and when I was a teen, there was an uprising."

"No." Much to my chagrin, Penelope pulls back, ending the hug, but I keep her hands clutched in mine and rest them on my lap.

"They tried to overthrow our family and take everything we'd built. An assassin snuck in one night and killed Dad.

With the help of Eleazer, Dad's second in command, Lucie took her place on the throne and eliminated all the traitors. I felt I owed it to her to stay until things were under control."

"So how did you end up here?"

"Demons don't have a wide range of emotions. Cruelty and malice are their bread and butter. I'm... *different*. I always have been. The human side of me made me feel things I shouldn't. Made me crave something... *more*. Something I couldn't find in Hell. I always thought it was a weakness—had I stayed in Hell, maybe it would have been."

"So you left?" She squeezes my hand, eyes brimming with hope.

"After 200 years in Hell, Lucie agreed to let me come to the surface. I think she was hoping it was a phase." I snicker. "If I could get the human urges out of my system, I'd come back and help her lead. But that was fifty years ago, and I have no intention of going back."

"Did you find what you were looking for?" Her eyes twinkle as they meet mine.

My chest warms, and I hook a finger under her chin. "I think so."

That blush is back, staining her cheeks when her eyes drop. She lightly pushes my hand away.

It's okay, sweetness. I can be patient.

Her bashfulness disappears in the next instant, replaced by a smug curl to her lush lips and a waggle of her delicate eyebrows. “So if Lucie is the queen, then that means you’re a princess?”

My fingers pinch the bridge of my nose as I snort a laugh. “Not you, too! No matter how much I scold him, Fenrir continues to call me princess. At this point, I think he’s only doing it to get a rise out of me.”

Penelope’s giggle makes sharing my past worth it. “Is that why you have Fenrir? He’s, like, your guard?”

I nod. “Sending him with me gave Lucie peace of mind, I guess. Not that he’d do any good.” I glance over the back of the couch to Penelope’s bedroom door, where Fen is no doubt still zonked out. If he’s not irritating me, he’s sleeping. “Alright, you saw my damage... and you’re still here.”

Pen blows out a breath that ruffles the stray hairs around her face. “A deal’s a deal. You promise not to judge?”

I draw an *X* over my heart with my finger. “Cross my heart, sweetness. I don’t think there’s anything that would make me not like you.”

Another snarky eye roll has me biting my lip to stop my smile. “*Fine*. You already know that I grew up in the Hamptons. Mom and Dad still live there, in the same house.”

I nod, recalling our unexpected run-in at the farmers’ market weeks ago, where I managed to get basic information out of her.

"I guess you'd say my family is well off. I'm self-aware enough to know I didn't want for anything as a child, at least not physically. Earning the love and attention I craved… that was a little harder to come by." Her eyes drop to her lap, and she picks at a thread on the blanket.

"Why?"

One shoulder lifts, then drops. "Dad's a high-profile defense attorney. For as long as I can remember, he's worked on big cases all over the country, so he wasn't around much when I was a kid. Sure, he'd pop in with a present after spending the week away. But he was oblivious to how Mom controlled nearly every aspect of my existence."

My fingers curl into a fist at the mention of her mom. I've never met the woman—Devil help her if I do—but I've been witness to the aftermath.

Pen must notice my unease, as her fingers uncurl mine and lace them with hers instead. "I know you're not her biggest fan."

"That's an understatement, sweetness."

She laughs, but quickly sobers. "As much as I tried to earn her love and meet her impossible standards when I was younger, I'm not entirely sure she's capable of unconditional love. You see, there's a big age gap between me and Colin, so sometimes I wonder if she even wanted me. Am I just a living doll she thinks she can play dress up with? What she thinks is love is commenting on my outfit or hairstyle choices. Setting me up on blind dates with 'prestigious suitors.'"

When her eyes meet mine, I search her face before nodding to give her the courage to forge on.

"When I was ten, I distinctly remember her forcing me to leave a friend's birthday party after I had a second helping of cake. My punishment was to walk on the treadmill for an hour and have nothing but broccoli for dinner that night."

There goes my hand again, curling into a fist around hers as my blood boils for a younger Penelope. "Your dad didn't stop her?"

Messy blonde hair wobbles in its bun when she shakes her head. "I think he was in California or Texas for a big case. I remember him calling at bedtime." Her eyes shimmer with unshed moisture, and she wipes her nose on her sleeve. "I had to choke back tears so he wouldn't suspect anything. As a ten-year-old, I thought if he found out, he would leave her... leave *us*. I didn't want to be responsible for ruining my family, so I never told anyone how cruel she was."

A single tear breaks free, cascading down her cheek before I can catch it. "Oh, sweet girl, I'm so sorry you had to carry that burden." I wipe away the next set of tears before they can stain her hoodie.

"She's always been critical of my appearance. After a while, I learned to stay out of her path as much as possible. To not make waves and keep quiet. It was better when she'd ignore me. Without Colin, I wouldn't have survived in that house. He took care of me when our parents didn't." A sad smile ghosts across her lips. "He made sure I had tampons and pads when I got my first period. He gave me the birds and the bees talk before my first date with Cory Anderson." Delicate shoulders ripple with a shudder. "He got a little too handsy when he dropped me off in his brand-new Jaguar his parents bought him for his sixteenth birthday."

"*Asshole*," I mutter, making Penelope laugh.

"Don't worry, I didn't give him the luxury of a second date."

The urge to touch her wins out, and I run a thumb over her cheekbone. The skin is warm and soft. "Smart girl."

"Colin was more of a parent than the people who gave me life. And now, he's married with his own kids."

"Is that something you want? Kids?" If she says yes, I'd move Hell and Earth to give her what she wants. *Slow down, Syn.*

She chews her bottom lip. "I used to, but now, I don't know. What if I turn out like her? What if I'm a horrible mother? A monster." She whispers the last part like it's a curse.

"Hey." I cup her face to keep her focus on me. "You could never treat a child like that, Pen. You're the nicest person I've ever met. You're sweet and pure. Any child would be lucky to have you as a mother."

"Thank you." Her voice cracks, moisture welling in the corners of her eyes again. "Maybe in the future, I'll want kids. But for now, I'm enjoying being unattached." She huffs a laugh. "I'd much rather focus on building myself up after years of being broken down by my mom."

"I think that sounds like a perfect plan... *after* we play hooky today." I wink and toss her the TV remote.

She clicks to one of the streaming apps before picking a movie. "You drive a hard bargain, Syn. A day rotting on the couch sounds amazing. I'm exhausted. And thank you again for taking care of me yesterday." Her eyes flit to the empty containers on the table before meeting mine again as she smiles. "And today."

"No thanks needed, sweetness. I see you, and I'm always here for you."

The delicate line of her throat bobs with a harsh swallow before she breaks eye contact, gaze focusing on the soft glow of the television screen.

Both of our emotions are running high, so it's not the time to confess how I really feel... and how much I want her to be mine. I'll stay in my lane as her friend for a little while longer.

What's another few days when I've been searching for her for decades?

Chapter 14

Synthea

My cheery whistle carries up the empty staircase, bouncing off the deep burgundy walls as I take the stairs two at a time. There's a pep in my combat boots, catapulting me toward my front door.

A sweet treat waits for me on the other side, like she has every night this week. My sweetness. Just the thought of her dimpled cheeks scrunched with a wide grin has me smiling.

And just like every other night recently, I dipped out of work at the Taproom a few hours early. Over the last week, I've found myself choosing to delegate more and more so I can be home when Penelope is.

Rafe and Frank have things under control. A pleasant surprise, Frank has actually been an unexpected godsend. Hardworking and charming, with his background in sales, he could sell snow to a polar bear shifter.

My whistle turns to a hum, tail swishing along to my happy tune, as I dig my keys from the pocket of my worn black jeans. We bared our souls to each other after her migraine, and ever since, she's been more open to spending time together.

In her head, we're friends. I, however, know the truth. She's mine. She just hasn't figured it out yet, too stuck on the judgement and rules of her mother.

But there are no rules when it comes to love. And I'll spend the rest of my days building her up until she realizes she was made for me... and I for her.

I twist my key into the lock before swinging the apartment door open. Instead of a pretty blonde waiting for me on the couch, I'm met by a silent, empty room—apart from Fenrir, who's passed out in his usual spot.

"Maybe she went out?" I murmur. Although, that's not like Penelope. Her pattern is predictable. Routine. Besides me dragging her to the farmers' market every Sunday, she's either at work or home. And I don't think she's gone out after dark since moving in.

My stomach drops, and before my body dives headfirst into fight-or-flight mode, I tug my phone from my pocket.

Thumbs flying across the screen, I pull up the text thread with Penelope from earlier tonight.

Sweetness: The contracts for the tattoo shop are finalized and waiting in your inbox. One last signature and the place is officially yours! I can't wait to see what you do with it!

In fact, the email reminder is waiting for me in my notifications.

Me: Working on a Friday night, sweetness? Take a break and come have a drink with me.

Sweetness: Can't. I'm leaving early tomorrow morning for my girls' weekend with Annie, Ness & Maggie. Still need to pack and get some sleep.

Her girls' trip. How could I forget? I've been so engrossed in soaking up every second with her that it completely slipped my mind.

Slinking down the dark hallway, I stop outside Penelope's closed door. Hand hanging by my side, I resist the urge to knock, instead continuing to my room, where I throw on some pajamas. AKA a threadbare cropped t-shirt and some knit shorts.

My body is buzzing with energy, bare feet pacing a line on the rug in front of my bed. I haven't seen Penelope all day. Besides the little note I left with her coffee this morning and the texts earlier, I haven't talked to her either.

...And I'm having withdrawals.

Pathetic. A centuries-old demon so far gone for a human that I can't even go twenty-four hours without seeing her.

Fuck it. Breaking from their path, my feet carry me out of my room and back to Penelope's door.

I'll just peek in and make sure she's okay.

Hand on the knob, a soft whimper hits my ears.

Every muscle in my body locks up. I dare not even breathe as I rest an ear against the wood and wait.

The faintest moan, followed by a rasped "Syn" comes through the closed door.

Is she touching herself while thinking of me? A self-satisfied grin curls my lips when another moan trickles into the dark hallway.

Throwing caution—and logical thought—to the wind, I tighten my hold on the doorknob and twist. Pushing into the room on silent feet, I almost swallow my tongue at what's waiting for me in the moonlit space.

Covers tangled around her ankles, Penelope writhes on the bed. The arch of her spine puts the small mounds of her tits on display for me to devour.

Visible through the thin fabric of her white tank top, the peaked buds have saliva pooling on my tongue.

Eyes shut and oblivious to my presence, Penelope's hand is nestled under her pale-blue panties. Hidden by her bent legs, I can only imagine how perfect and wet her fingers are as they slide over her clit before thrusting into her cunt.

Fuck. Arousal blooming low in my belly, my body lights up as I step closer.

"Please." Her voice is slightly pained, bottom lip trapped under her teeth.

Her free hand clutches at her tit, squeezing the flesh in a rough grip.

I should feel bad for spying on her in such a vulnerable moment, but the waves of lust rippling off her have caught me in their grasp. Addictive. Suffocating. I don't think I could leave this room even if I wanted to.

And I don't. At least, not until I see my sweetness out of her mind with pleasure.

So, like the predator I am, I stalk to the end of the bed. Beneath the thin fabric of her underwear, Penelope's fingers twist and turn.

Her eyes are still shut, allowing me to look my fill.

A frustrated noise leaves her mouth. "Not again. I'm so close."

Ah, can she not make herself come?

I'm playing with fire when I place a knee onto the mattress, using all the care in the world not to disturb her. The center of the cotton between her legs is damp.

Oh, fuck. Movements slow and calculated, I climb onto the bed, lean forward, and suck in a breath. Penelope's sweet musk fills my lungs, choking me as I inhale.

She smells so fucking good.

I might die if I don't get to see her.

Taste her.

Abruptly, Penelope rips her hand out of her underwear. At the sudden movement, I tense, but she curls her fingers into a fist and pounds the mattress.

"Why does this happen every time?" Sexual frustration oozes from her voice.

And I speak before I can think better of it. "Need some help, sweetness?"

Baby blue eyes spring wide, and Penelope scoots onto her elbows. "S-Syn. What are you doing in here?"

I smirk. "It looks like you could use some help." My eyes drop to the damp patch on her panties.

"I-I... Wha— W-We can't." There's no conviction behind her stuttered attempt.

I arch an eyebrow. "Why not? You need to come, and I bet I can get you there."

Her throat clicks with a swallow, but the wet spot between her spread thighs grows larger, her nectar soaking the flimsy fabric. She also hasn't covered her body or asked me to leave. She wants this as much as I do.

"I won't touch you," I promise, sitting back to give her some space.

For all my bravado, I'm still shocked when she bites her bottom lip and nods.

Play it cool. This might be your only opportunity.

Even if it ruins our friendship and the nice little living arrangement we have, I'm too selfish to stop. Not after getting a hit of her sweet scent.

"You're sure?" *Stupid mouth! Just make her come. Don't ask questions!*

Penelope nods again. "I'm sure. It's been weeks since I've been able to make myself... you know." She dips her chin, and a rush of color fills her cheeks.

"Orgasm, sweetness?"

"Y-Yeah," she croaks.

"Don't worry. I'll take care of you. I don't want you hurting, baby girl. Can I see you?" I nod to the fabric covering her delicious cunt. "I won't touch... I promise."

Fingers hooking into the sides of her underwear, Penelope lifts her hips and slides them down her legs.

I may actually be dead. Death by Penelope's gorgeous pussy. Before I can drown in it, I gulp down the pool of saliva that's filled my mouth, eyes devouring the treasure between her legs. Golden curls lead the way to glistening pink folds. Her clit is engorged and waiting to be licked and sucked—*not right now. No touching, remember?*

Stupid. Why did I say I wouldn't touch her?

"Syn? Are you okay?" Loose blonde waves cascade down her chest, and her rosy nipples peek through her tank top.

As much as I hate to, I drag my eyes up to hers. "You're stunning, baby girl."

The flush from her cheeks spreads down to her heaving chest. What I wouldn't give to see her perky tits unclothed, but I'm not about to push my luck.

"Put your fingers on your clit, sweetness. Show me how you like to be touched."

My chest swells when she obeys and gently places her right hand between her thighs. Her movements are hesitant, unsure eyes flicking to mine.

Is Penelope Martin a virgin?

This doesn't seem like the time or place to ask. Instead, I drop my voice to a seductive rasp. "That's my good girl. Add a little more pressure."

A second later, Penelope lets out the most intoxicating moan I've ever heard. The sound has arousal soaking my own panties. Fuck, I want her so bad. My fingers curl into the rumpled sheets. Not touching her is killing me.

"If you think that feels good, press a finger into your perfect cunt, Penelope. Fuck yourself for me."

She does. Flipping her wrist, her thumb stays on her clit as her middle finger drives deep inside her.

My gaze follows her movements. Stretched around the single digit, her opening glistens, begging to be filled and fucked with my fingers or feasted upon by my mouth. "Do you know how badly I want to taste you? All this sweet nectar dripping from your pretty cunt."

"Do it," she sobs, hips writhing against her fingers.

"I don't think you understand, sweetness. If I do, I won't be able to stop, and you'd be mine. So tempting. So innocent. I should leave you here, a sobbing mess waiting for the release only I can deliver."

She adds a second finger and thrusts at a faster pace. Her free hand snakes between her legs to take up the job of strumming her clit. "Please, no."

Careful not to touch her beautiful flesh, I shuffle closer, until I'm kneeling between her spread legs and my hands hover over her hips. "But I won't." Overwhelmed by her lust and mine, my shadows uncurl from my body. One slinks up to her face and pushes her sweaty hair back from her forehead. "That's not my style, sweet girl. I prefer to give you orgasm after orgasm, until you're limp and sated."

Penelope whimpers, fingers pushing her closer and closer to her peak.

"Mark my words, Penelope, next time, I *will* touch you."

"Please. I'm so close." Her back arches, and her thigh muscles tighten.

"I'll fill all your holes with shadows and tail while I suck your sweet little clit until you're screaming my name."

"Don't stop," she cries, fingers strumming her clit faster. Arousal drips from her opening, down the crack of her ass, to her pulsing back hole.

Damn, I can't wait to put my tail in that tight hole while I eat her cunt. At the thought, my tail flicks against the mattress. I bet she'd beg and beg for me to let her come over and over again.

Quivering thighs bracket me, and it takes all my restraint not to drag my fingers up her legs, grip her hips, and bring her succulent pussy to my mouth so I can feast. Instead, I fall forward, bracing myself on my hands at the last second, bringing me face to face with lust-drunk azure eyes.

Penelope gasps, but her fingers never stop playing with her perfect cunt. She's right there... teetering on the edge of bliss.

Ghosting my nose along her jaw, her panted breaths ruffle my hair. My lips find her ear as she tips her head back on a moan, spine arching off the bed.

"That's it. Come for me, sweetness," I whisper against the shell of her ear as she tumbles into oblivion and cries out her release.

Heavy lids droop as she mumbles, "Thank you."

When her breathing evens out and her eyes don't re-open, I know she's fallen asleep. "Good night, sweetness. Next time, I will be touching you." And there will be a next time.

With great reluctance, I climb off the bed. I don't want to leave her, but this is different from the night she had a migraine and asked me to stay. Penelope didn't ask for any of this, and—as much as I hate to admit it—she might regret her decision in the morning.

I need to give her space. But before I do, I drag the sheet over her, lean in, and brush my lips against her forehead. The skin is warm and slightly salty with sweat. *Delicious.* When I pull back, I brush my fingers through her hair, drawing out the touch before I straighten to leave.

It'll have to tide me over until she lets me in again.

Pale blue fabric on the floor snags my attention, and I bend to snatch her panties from the rug. Bringing them to my nose, I inhale. The scent permeates my pores and sparks a pulsing need between my legs.

With lust clouding my vision, I stumble to my room and flop onto my bed, ripping my shorts and panties off in the process. I'm primed to explode, inner walls clenching around nothing as my tail vibrates to life, finding its home on my clit.

"Fuck, yes," I moan as tremors rush through the bejeweled sensitive bundle of nerves. One drunken night with Rafe, and he convinced me to pierce my clit.

Totally worth it.

I shrug off my shirt and twist my pierced nipples. Another wave of pleasure ripples through me.

The bedroom door is wide open. Anyone—okay, *someone* in particular—could wander in and catch me.

Hell, I hope she does.

A shadowy tendril slithers across the mattress, wrapping itself around Penelope's used panties and bringing them to my face. I inhale again, bathing my senses in her. Fifty years, I've waited for this beautiful creature, and in the seconds she lost herself in pleasure, she revealed just how much she was made for me.

Another dark thread sprouts from my body and weaves around my thigh before thrusting into my weeping core. The sheer force of being impaled sends my back into an arc, thrusting my tits to the ceiling. I moan, remembering how impeccably Penelope obeyed my commands. Her body responded to each depraved word in a way I could only dream of.

A second shadow twists around the first, creating a thicker appendage. I groan at the burning stretch of my inner muscles as it pistons inside me. "Fuck," I moan, head tipped back onto the pillows. "I'm gonna come."

My tail slaps against my clit. Once. Twice. Three times. And I fucking shatter into a million microscopic pieces as nirvana overtakes me.

When I finally come down from my high, the panties are clutched in my fist. I sag against the mattress, wishing the space beside me was filled with my little human. In the morning, if Penelope regrets what we did, I don't know if I'll be able to let her go.

Chapter 15

Penelope

I flip back the sheets again—for the hundredth time—but my underwear is nowhere to be found. My knees connect with the plush rug, and I peek under the bed... *again*.

"Where did they go?" Standing, I ball my hands and place them on my hips.

I've been awake, body thrumming with energy, since five a.m. On a Saturday, that should be a crime, but my brain won't shut off. Playing and replaying what happened last night on some sort of sadistic loop.

She made me come.

Harder than I ever have before.

Without even touching me.

Since moving in, my body has been in a near-constant state of arousal because of a certain purple-haired demon princess. And no matter how many times I tried to use my fingers to bring myself relief, it never worked.

Until Syn came into my room last night and sent me tumbling over the edge with her words alone.

Did I ruin everything, though?

What if she wants to do it again?

What if she doesn't?

I can't think about that now, or I'll be a twitching, pacing ball of nerves the entire weekend.

After getting dressed, I spent the last half hour looking for my darn panties. I'm almost 100 percent certain I threw them on the floor in my haste to get Syn's eyes on me, but they weren't there this morning.

My phone buzzes where it sits on top of my weekender bag.

Maggie: Be there in 30!

Time to face the music.

"It'll be fine. Just act normal." Moisture dampens my jean shorts as I swipe my sweaty palm along my hip. Clutching the straps of my bag, I empty my lungs before filling them again and leaving the safety of my bedroom.

Down the hall, Syn's bedroom door is open. Sunlight spills into the hallway through the open curtains. She's already awake. So much for avoiding an awkward run-in.

Come on, big girl panties, don't fail me now.

Plastering on a wide smile, I affix my mask and enter the open kitchen and living room area.

"Morning, sweetness," Syn says from her place at the kitchen table. Beside her plate of eggs, bacon, and hash browns is a second, along with a mug of coffee. "I wasn't sure what time you were leaving, but your door was shut when I got up."

"Maggie will be here in about half an hour."

"Will you have breakfast with me? I think we should talk about last night." She tips her head to the chair next to hers.

I swallow the bile rising in my throat, set my bag on the couch, and take a seat next to her.

Over the rim of her mug, dark eyes track my movements as I stab a piece of egg and bring it to my mouth.

"Are you a virgin?"

Fork clattering to the plate, I choke. "What?! No!"

A warm hand lands on my back, and Syn rubs circles with the perfect calming pressure. "Hey, it's okay. I'm not judging. It just seemed like you were having trouble last night."

My cheeks heat at the memory of her between my spread thighs, midnight gaze locked on my most intimate parts. I don't think anyone has ever looked at me like that before. Like they wanted to *devour* me. "I've, um, been with a few men. But I've never orgasmed with any of them."

It's Syn's turn to be shocked. On a gasp, her eyes widen. "*Never.*"

I shake my head, gaze dropping to my plate. "It's hard for me to stay in the moment. My mind wanders, and I get distracted. Usually, I just go through the motions until they finish." I clear my throat. "It's not a big deal."

Syn scoffs. "It most certainly is. Sex shouldn't be one sided. It's about mutual satisfaction. What about masturbation?"

I shrug, somehow gaining the courage to meet her eyes again. There's no judgement in them, only a spark of curiosity. "You saw what happened last night. It takes too long, so I gave up."

"Even with toys or vibrators?"

"Mom was strict. And by the time I lived on my own, I never bothered."

A sensual smirk takes over her face, which leaves mine hot to the touch when I rest a hand on my cheek. "We're going to have to remedy this situation immediately."

"Why?"

Her hand lands on my thigh, sending a rush of goosebumps scattering over the bare flesh. "Because, sweetness, everyone deserves pleasure."

My brow crinkles in the middle. "You don't regret what we did last night?"

"No." A singular word. Determined and confident. It should make me less confused, but it only adds to the thoughts swirling in my head.

It'd be so easy to forget everything I know and jump back into bed with Syn, but Mom's whispering voice in the back of my mind has me thinking otherwise.

Syn's lips tic downward and her dark eyebrows lower when I push her hand off my leg. "What's wrong, sweetness?"

"I'm confused. All my life, I've been taught that I should be with a man. That's what's right. That's what's expected. *Normal*. I've been forced to live by my mother's rules. But now I don't know anymore."

"What if there are no rules, baby girl?" She says it with a nonchalance that has me wanting to believe her, but I can't.

"Isn't what we did wrong?"

This time, Syn laces her fingers through mine so I can't brush her off. "According to whom? Your mother?"

My gaze drops to our joined hands. Gray against tan. Black stiletto nails against short naked ones.

She's everything I'm not. Fearless. Sensual. *Strong*.

Not weak, like me. Can't even stand up to my own mom and take control of my life. I gulp, not able to face the hope in her eyes. "Can you give me some time? Some space?"

I follow with my eyes as she brings our hands to her lips, placing a featherlight kiss on each knuckle. "Of course. I would never force you into anything you don't want, Penelope. But I like you."

"I like you, too. What I feel when I'm around you"—I sigh—"it's not like anything I've experienced before. The flutters. The excitement." I smile, and Syn matches it with one of hers. If only it were that easy. If only I could shut out Mom's words and fear of her judgement. "Ugh." I rub a circle on my temple. "My head is a mess."

A soft buzz in my pocket breaks the moment. Pulling out my phone, I find a message from Maggie. "They're here." I hold the screen up for her to see.

"Go. Talk to your friends. See what kind of wisdom they can give you, and I'll be here when you get back." Then, in a move that makes me want to skip the whole weekend, Syn's thumb brushes my jaw and her lips land on my cheek. "No matter what you decide."

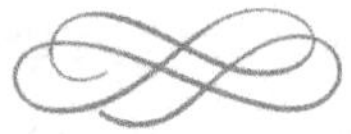

"Hey." Annie plops down in the sand next to me. "You okay?"

Eyes lingering on the horizon as the sun dips below the waterline, I wrap my arms around my bent legs. "I'm fine."

"You've been quiet all day." Her claw-tipped fingers twirl a seashell, but her golden eyes stay on me. "You sure there's not something on your mind?"

Resting my cheek on one knee, I meet her gaze. "Do you remember brunch a few weeks ago?"

Annie nods. "Sure. Does this have something to do with this woman you're having feelings for?"

My gut tightens. If there's anyone who would understand what I'm going through, it's Annie. She hated Cyrus before they ended up together. Somehow, she was able to set her own feelings aside and look at the big picture. Maybe she can help *me* see the big picture. "Yes."

"And how does she feel about the situation?"

Syn has made it abundantly clear, time and time again, how she feels about me. It's me. I'm the problem. Me and my stupid brain. "She's all in."

Annie's lips purse, eyebrows dropping low. "So... what's the problem?"

"*Me*. I was raised with certain expectations. Certain beliefs. But my feelings for Syn have me questioning everything. She makes me happy, and she makes me feel seen. She takes care of me and builds me up." For the first time in a long time, I'm not just going through the motions of my life. Instead, I'm alive and excited for each day.

And it's because of Syn.

Annie smiles. "Those are all good things."

I drag a finger through the sand. It's still warm from the earlier summer sun. "But there's this overwhelming guilt that I'm doing something wrong. That being with a woman is wrong."

"And where is that guilt coming from?"

"My mom. My entire life, she's been trying to mold me into something that I'm not. She's the one who's been setting me up on those awful dates all summer."

Annie scoffs. "Dreadful woman."

"For as long as I can remember, she's told me I'd grow up, marry a man, and have babies. That's what's expected of me.... but I don't want those things." Moisture springs to my eyes as my voice drops to a whisper. "And I'm afraid once she actually listens and realizes that I'm not her perfect little doll, that she'll hate me."

A warm arm wraps around me, and Annie drags me into her side. "Oh, Pen."

I sniffle and wipe my nose. "It's stupid. She wasn't the best mom, but I still love her. Even after everything she's put me through."

"Honey, your emotions aren't stupid. If you want to be with Syn, then be with Syn. Love doesn't come in one shape or size; that's the beauty of it."

"But what about—"

She holds up a finger. "Uh ah. If your mother can't see that, then with all due respect, fuck her. You have a house full of people up there"—she glances over her shoulder at the beach rental—"who would go to bat for you, Pen. Without hesitation."

For some reason, the words finally click. My happiness is more important than my mom's expectations. She wouldn't really disown me for loving someone different than she expected, right?

What kind of parent would do that?

I can't think about that now.

New resolve flows through my veins. If I choose to be weak and kneel to Mom yet again, I could be missing out on something that makes me irrationally happy.

"Do you think Ness and Maggie would be mad if I head back to the city right now?"

Annie bumps my shoulder with hers. "No, honey. Go get your girl!"

Consequences be damned, it's time to do something selfish. Something wholly for me. As the sun sets over the Atlantic, and I run up the beach to the back door, it feels like the start of something new. It's terrifying and utterly exhilarating.

Chapter 16

Synthea

A low whine comes from in front of the apartment door. It's the second in a matter of minutes. "Relax, Fen. She'll be back tomorrow."

Clearly, my words go in one big ear and out the other as he continues to pace. Toenails click on the floor and his tail swishes from side to side.

Sighing, I lean back on the couch. The credits roll for whatever rom-com I put on earlier.

Truth be told, it's not just Fen. I've been on edge since Penelope left, too.

Will she find the clarity she needs? Or was giving her space a mistake?

You can't force her to love you, Syn.

In hopes of distracting myself, I pick up the remote and start the movie over again. It's not like I was paying attention the first time anyway.

Finally getting with the program, Fen hops onto the couch beside me. I scoot out of the way at the last second when he lays down so I don't end up under the massive furball. He lets out another whine before resting his head on his front paws, red eyes fixed on the front door.

"What am I? Chopped liver? Penelope moves in, and you act like I don't exist." I bury my hand into the fur on his hip, giving it a thorough scratch.

Over his shoulder, he rolls his eyes and huffs. "*You provide sustenance and walks, but the cupcake is nicer.*"

My mouth falls open on a scoff, but my response dies on my tongue when a key slips into the lock.

Deserting me like the traitor he is, Fen bolts from the couch as the front door swings open. Golden ponytail swinging down her back, Penelope drops her bag on the floor and kneels in front of Fen, who takes up whining again while his tail smacks against the ground.

"I wasn't gone *that* long," she says between giggles when he licks the side of her face and knocks her onto her ass. "I missed you, too, Fen." When she wraps her arms around his furry neck, and he rests his head on her shoulder, I just about die.

I never thought I'd find someone like Penelope to brighten my life, but here she is... loving my persnickety hellhound and all.

Leaving Fen at the door, there's determination burning in her blue eyes as she makes a beeline for me.

One leg on either side of mine, her weight lands in my lap, sending my heart into a frenzy.

She's here. She came back.

Soft hands cup my cheeks, and I'm helpless to the flames raging in her gaze as she leans close and murmurs, "I want to be with you, Syn. So much."

Did I hear her right? Or have I finally lost the plot and my brain is playing tricks on me?

I have been teleporting more than usual lately. Maybe it's rattled a few wires loose upstairs.

"Wait." I brace a hand on her chest, halting her until her lips hover just a breath away. Juicy and tempting. In a cadence that matches mine, her heart gallops beneath the skin. "You really want to be with me?

She nods, confidence gripping her voice when she says, "Yes, Syn. I'm choosing this—*you*—for me. It's my turn to be selfish."

The next instant, her lips are on mine. Shock and awe war inside me as she initiates the kiss.

I've spent far too long imagining what it would be like to kiss my sweetness.

And, let me tell you, the fantasy is nowhere near as good as the real thing.

What starts as a meek press of her mouth against mine turns into an all-out inferno. I nearly burst into flames when Penelope sinks her hands into my hair, pulling me closer.

My fingers land on her hips, tightening their grip when her tongue curls around mine, and she moans.

I should stop her. Make sure she's 100% certain of her decision, but the selfish part of me has waited months for this moment and doesn't want to stop.

Fuck it. Selfish Syn wins. "Hang on, sweetness," I mumble against her lips before standing from the couch. My hands slip to cup her denim-covered ass, wishing more than anything I had her bare cheeks in my palms. *Soon*.

Continuing to maul my mouth like she doesn't need oxygen, Penelope secures her legs around my waist as my strides carry us to my bedroom.

Together, we tumble onto the bed, lost to the heated duel of our mouths.

Demanding fingers leave my hair to tug at the hem of my shirt. They turn frantic when they coast over my sides, leaving a trail of warmth as the fabric is pushed over my face. We're forced to break our kiss, and Penelope giggles when my horns get stuck in the neckhole.

I wasn't expecting her to be back until tomorrow, so I opted for a baggy t-shirt and comfy boyshorts.

"Off. Now." The impatient whine in her voice has me chuckling as I maneuver my horns through and fling the shirt to the side.

No longer obscured by pesky fabric, my gaze locks on Penelope as hers rakes over me. Hesitant, she raises her fingers, which shake slightly when they hover over the golden ink between my breasts. "You're beautiful," she whispers.

Bracing my weight on my hands, I circle her wrist with my tail and bring her fingers to my skin. The jolt of pleasure from a simple touch has a tremble rushing down my spine, and I moan. "I'm yours, sweetness. Touch me."

My words spur her on. Palm flattening against my flesh, she cups my breast. Another burst of delight when her thumb brushes the hoop bisecting my nipple. "Is this okay?" The question lingers in her eyes when they rise to mine.

Shifting my weight to one hand, I cup her cheek and grin. "It'd be better if you were naked."

Her fingers leave me, going to the bottom of her tank top.

Lightning fast, I straddle her, grip both her wrists, and slam them against the mattress.

Penelope gasps. This position leaves her totally helpless but, surprisingly, she doesn't fight my hold. I lean down until my lips nestle against the shell of her ear. "Now, now, sweetness." I tsk. "I've been waiting for this moment since the night we met. You're not about to ruin it for me. Understand?"

Her pulse gallops when I run my nose down the flesh of her neck, but she nods. "Yes."

"Good." Sitting back, I trail my finger down the center of her body. Hands still above her head, her back arches to follow the movement. Fuck, she responds so perfectly. "Keep those there." I nod to her curling and uncurling fingers.

"O-Okay," she says before digging her teeth into her lower lip.

My fingers toy with the hem of her tank top. "You enjoyed the other night, right?"

Her head bobs up and down, pupils expanding to overtake the bright blue of her irises.

At a pace that's meant to torture us both, I drag the fabric up until her belly button is on display. Goosebumps break out across her abdomen when I lean down and kiss her adorable navel. "Then, I promise, you'll enjoy what I have planned for you right now."

In response, Penelope's thighs squeeze together, legs scissoring subtly in a chase to relieve the arousal likely coursing through her system.

I inch the fabric higher until her breasts pop free. Not restrained by a bra, the dusky pink peaks of her nipples stand to attention. Her breasts are small, but perky. Perfect.

And they have me salivating.

When I lean down and suck one of the beaded tips into my mouth, Penelope's chest reverberates with a low moan. "Do you like that, sweetness?" Switching to the other tit, I drag my tongue over the sensitive bud before nipping it with my teeth.

"Yesss," she hisses.

I caution a glance up at her face and find her eyes pinched shut. Blonde eyebrows dip together like she's concentrating on not letting the pleasure slip through her fingers.

Don't worry, sweetness, I'll make sure you get yours. Multiple times.

A trail of saliva follows my tongue and lips as I lick, suck, and kiss my way down her body. Making sure it gets the attention it deserves, my tongue dives into her belly button before I close my teeth on the flesh below it.

Penelope's ribs flare as her stomach caves, and she sucks in a gasp.

"Still feel good?" My eyes travel over the creature laid out before me. She's radiant. Skin flushed a brilliant shade of rose. Chest heaving. Whimpers and moans spilling from her lips.

"Y-Yes." Penelope's fingers curl into the sheets above her head like she wants to touch me, but she also wants to obey my earlier command.

"You'll tell me if I do something you don't like?"

She nods. "Yes."

"Good girl," I whisper. The sultry rasp of my voice has my sweet human trembling. Beneath me, her hips twist as much as they can under my weight. She's right where I want her... aching for something only I can provide.

Rising to my knees, I pop the button on her denim shorts. The sound of the zipper when I tug it down has Penelope scrambling onto her elbows, eyes glued to my hands as I grip the waist of her shorts and panties. Slowly, I peel them down her thighs.

After some shuffling, I finally have my sweetness wholly naked, spread out like a feast for me on my bed. My hands run up and down her outer thighs. She's fucking stunning. Soft and smooth. And so damn warm. If I'm not careful, I could get lost in all her silky skin and luscious curves.

Somebody pinch me. Is this real life?

"Has anyone ever eaten this pretty cunt, baby girl?" Two dark tendrils unfurl from my body as I await her answer.

"N-No." By now, her cheeks are burning bright. From embarrassment or arousal, I'm not sure. The color spreads down her neck and chest in a blotchy mess that I want to trace with my tongue. "Umm... W-What does it feel like?"

I hold in my chuckle, but a Cheshire Cat grin overtakes my lips. "Oh, sweet Penelope. Would you like me to show you?" Like two midnight pythons, my shadows slither around each thigh and spread her legs wider.

Arousal glistens on her plump cunt lips. Still wrapped around her thighs, my shadows crawl over the sheets until they wind around her wrists, too.

Fuck. She looks exquisite wrapped in my darkness. Trussed up like a prize boar, ready for the taking.

Ready to be feasted upon.

All I need is a single word, a single yes, and I'll devour her.

"Yes." Her whispered consent snaps the last mangled thread of restraint I've kept from fraying... until now.

My fingers dent the supple flesh of her ass as I raise her lower half off the bed. Bending down, I run my nose through her folds, suffocating myself on her sweet musk.

Tongue following suit, I lick from her rear pucker to her clit. "Oh, fuuuuck," I moan before repeating my path.

Sweet and salty. Like a salted caramel cupcake.

The taste lingers on my tongue, causing an ache to bloom deep in my core. I've had numerous partners throughout my lifetime, but no one has turned me into a simpering mess like this human.

I can't wait to watch her orgasm again. To tip over the cliff's edge and freefall into a raging river of pleasure.

Above me, Penelope whimpers. Her thighs tug at their shadowy restraints, but I continue to hold her hostage, funneling my tongue and diving straight to the source.

Feeling a little left out, my tail slinks around my body, drawn to Penelope's clit like a damn magnet. It jolts, vibrating against her slick bundle of nerves.

"Oh!" Her squeak of surprise turns into a moan as I apply more pressure. "Ohhhh, my... that feels so good."

Mouth glued to her cunt, I chuckle.

The only thing that would make this moment better is her hands on me. In my hair. Grasping my horns for dear life.

So I loosen the shadows around her wrists, silent permission for her to touch as she pleases.

It works. A blink of an eye later, fingers sift through my hair, tangling near the roots and forcing my mouth tighter to her cunt. Of course, I go willingly, thrusting my tongue as far as I can inside her.

"Please don't stop. I'm so close." Between heaved breaths, her voice is frantic. Desperate. Her free hand clamps onto one of my longer horns as she rocks her hips against my face.

In a move that's sure to send her spiraling into orgasm, I shove my tail inside her tight channel. Curling against the front wall of her cunt, I ramp up the vibrations and seal my mouth to her clit, lashing it with my tongue.

Penelope nearly levitates off the bed when her back arches and she lets out an ear-splitting moan. Her inner muscles choke my tail, but I manage to keep the vibrations going until she collapses onto the mattress.

Unfurling from her thighs, my shadows retract into my body as I gently lay her lower half back on the bed. "You okay, sweetness?"

Eyes closed, she nods.

"Can you let go of my horn?" I tap her wrist.

She sits up, eyes springing wide and cheeks flaming. "Oh." Uncurling her fingers, her hand falls to her lap. "Sorry."

When her head drops, it's like a punch to the gut.

I hate when she shrinks herself. My sweetness is a radiant goddess who deserves to take up space—so much fucking space—in this world.

And I'm going to prove it to her, no matter how long it takes.

I hook a finger under her chin and guide those ethereal azure eyes to me. "You never have to apologize for touching me, Penelope. I like your hands on me… everywhere." In hopes of seeing the lust in her gaze explode, I add a wink.

It works.

Bursting with fireworks, her eyes skim down my body to the wet patch on the front of my panties. Yeah, that's the effect she has on me. "C-Could I touch you? Make you feel good?"

After pressing a kiss to her lips, I flop onto my back among the mountain of pillows. I like a good decorative pillow, okay?

"I'd never deny you anything, sweetness."

Chapter 17

Penelope

The warm smile on Syn's face should boost my confidence, but I've never done this before.

Up until about twenty minutes ago, I'd never even kissed a woman, let alone gone down on one.

Kneeling between her spread thighs, I peer up at the demon who just rocked my world. I'm pretty sure the haze of my orgasm is the only reason I have any confidence right now. My hands shake as I rest them on Syn's legs. *Hopefully, she doesn't notice how clammy they are.* "Will you tell me what to do?"

A bout of nerves twists my insides. I want to please her. *No*. I *need* to please her. Bring her the same pleasure she gave me.

Syn sits up, stroking a long finger along my jaw. The gesture has me quivering. “Relax for me, sweetness. I’ll tell you what to do.”

I nod, her words quelling the waves in my gut.

“Good girl. Now, take off my underwear.” She arches an eyebrow at the light gray fabric covering her lower body. There’s a noticeable damp patch on the front. Did I do that to her? Get her so aroused that she’s soaked her panties?

She certainly had me wet, hot, and bothered with the infuriatingly and torturously slow pace she undressed me.

In fact, the thought alone has another gush of arousal leaking from my core.

My body has never lit up like this for anyone. Does that mean I’m a lesbian? Or is it simply *her?*

Focus, Penelope. You have a very naked, sexy-as-sin demon waiting for you to go down on her. This isn’t the time for an existential crisis.

Pushing those thoughts aside, I slip my fingers under the waistband and slide the fabric down her slim hips and toned thighs. Syn isn’t curvy, like me, but her lithe, muscular body exudes power and sensuality, nonetheless.

Something I envy after years of shrinking to fit someone else’s ideals.

Syn would never make herself smaller or more palatable to please someone else.

Instead of letting myself spiral, I focus on the patch of dark curls between her thighs and absorb every drop of lust that she emanates, letting it build me up.

I've never gone down on a woman before... What if I do it wrong?

"Sweetness." Syn sits up again, and this time, she pulls me onto her lap. "We don't have to do this."

I shake my head, focusing on the dark orbs of her eyes. "I want to make you feel good. I just, ummm... what if I do it wrong?" Admitting my fear lifts a weight off my chest.

Warm laughter puffs against my mouth when she gives them a quick peck. "I promise, I'll enjoy every second of your lips and tongue on me. Just relax and listen to my voice."

After a final slow, drugging kiss, she lays back against the pillows. Her hand slips to her core, pulling the lips apart to reveal a purple gem nestled at the top.

I don't even know where to start, so I dive in, face first—literally. A metallic tang fills my mouth when I drag my tongue over the piercing, which has Syn's back arching and a moan spilling from her lips.

"Yesss," she hisses. "Right there."

So I do it again. And again. And again.

Until her tart cherry bourbon flavor engulfs every taste bud and her thighs tremble beside my ears.

I think she likes that.

"Fuck, sweetness. You're a natural."

The praise has warmth building in my chest as I suck her clit between my lips.

"Good girl. Just like that. You don't need to be shy. Add a few fingers, too."

Obeying her gentle instruction, I swipe two fingers through the trail of arousal leaking from her before sliding them into her opening. Like I would do to myself, I hook them against the front wall and stroke.

Sharp nails drag through my hair, fisting at the roots with a zip of pain. Syn moans when I curl my fingers again. "Keep doing that, sweetness, and you'll have me gushing in no time."

I want that. To taste every drop of her release and let her consume me.

Between sucking her clit and fingering her opening, I find a rhythm that has her thighs pinning to the sides of my head like earmuffs, the muscles going taut as her inner walls strangle my fingers.

"Oh *fuck*, add a third, sweetness," Syn moans.

I chance a glance up at her, finding black lava staring back at me, a wicked curve to her lips.

"Isn't that too much?"

She chuckles. "I can handle it. And give me your other hand."

One hand buried in her glistening pussy, I drop my weight to my elbow and extend my free hand. Syn directs my fingers to brush over the metal bar bisecting her beaded nipple.

Acting on instinct alone, I pinch the pebbled flesh as I slide a third finger into her. A wave of goosebumps rushes over her flesh. Head tipping back against the pillows, she moans.

Maybe I am a natural at this.

As more confidence inflates me, I roll and tug her nipple in time with the curling thrusts of my fingers. Too awestruck by her writhing body and sensuous cries, I don't notice her tail slip onto her clit until it roars to life a few inches in front of my face.

That must be the magic piece that pushes her over the edge because Syn's back bows into a harsh arch, her wailing moan cracks through the air like thunder, and her inner walls clamp down on my fingers to the point I can barely move them.

Frozen in place, mouth agape, all I can do is watch as the wave goes out to sea and her body relaxes onto the bed.

"H-How was it?" I dare to ask when a sated grin curves her mouth.

"It was perfect. You're perfect." Faster than I can blink, she sits up and wraps a hand around my throat, drawing my lips to hers. "I think I might be addicted to you, sweetness."

My hand slips from the heat between her thighs, landing on the bed next to her hip when I catch my weight, but my tongue slides against hers, soaking up the mix of our unique flavors. "I think I'm addicted to you, too." Pulling back, my smile matches hers, and it's like I'm floating on a cloud of bliss. I've never felt this light before. My head has never been this quiet.

I just hope it lasts, and it's not the quiet before the inevitable storm.

Needing the calm to last a bit longer, I ask, "Is it okay if I sleep in here tonight?"

Syn's chuckle rumbles through my body when she wraps her arms around me. "Did you think I was going to let you sleep anywhere but right here after you gave me the best orgasm of my life?"

I roll my eyes. "Come on. Let's get cleaned up."

After a quick rinse in the shower, I crawl under the covers and rest my head on Syn's chest. The steady *lub-dub* of her heart eases the anxious voices saying how this is too good to be true, how it will all blow up in my face.

My fingers trace the shimmering golden ink on her sternum. The smooth curve of the moth's wing leads to the jagged edges of the flames that surround it. "Does this mean I'm gay?" Fingers pausing, the question is out of my mouth before I can stop it. "Or bisexual? I've only been with men until tonight... Well, the other night, I guess. I don't actually know if I was attracted to any of the men

I dated, and I'm not really attracted to any other women. Only you. And—" A finger lands on my lips, quieting me, and I meet laughter-filled eyes.

"Breathe, Pen."

I blow out a breath around her finger, then fill my lungs again.

Leaving my mouth, her finger grazes along my jaw until it sifts into my hair with the others. Her head dips until her forehead rests against mine. "You don't have to figure it all out right now. And you don't have to figure it out alone, either, but it sounds like you might be pansexual."

I melt into her touch and the warmth of her body beneath mine. "What's that?"

Her fingertips knead my scalp, and I stifle a moan. "Essentially, you're attracted to someone based on their personality, regardless of their gender."

"I guess that makes sense. I mean, all of my past relationships have been with men, but I was friends with them before I felt comfortable taking that step to something romantic. Same with us. We were friends first."

Her snicker catches me off guard. "That's where you're wrong. We were never friends, sweetness. I just let you think we were so you didn't freak out." She bops the tip of my nose, and I scrunch it before knocking her hand away.

I huff, but there's no real anger behind it. "Whatever."

Syn tips my face to hers, the humor in her eyes melting into a raging fire of longing. "It's hearts, not parts, sweetness. And when I'm around you, I'm afraid my heart might beat right out of my chest."

As if agreeing with her, mine gallops like a stampede of wild stallions. "Me, too."

Please, don't let this end badly.

Chapter 18

Syn's chest rises with a breath before a snore leaves her mouth. I stifle a laugh, but continue watching her sleep.

Watching someone sleep after you had the best sex of your life isn't creepy, right?

Definitely not creepy.

Purple hair, sticking up in every direction, halos her face. Another snore ruffles a strand that hangs over her forehead. My gaze drags down her body, where the sheets are pooled around her waist, leaving her beautiful chest on display.

A rush of warmth spreads over me as I linger on the metal bars in her nipples. The gold ink etched into her skin shimmers under the morning sunlight as it streams through the window opposite the bed. I must really be bisexual or... what did Syn call it? Pansexual? Because I've never felt this all-consuming need to be around someone like I feel with her.

Sure, she's beautiful, but it's deeper than that. She sees me for who I am—or, at least, who I want to be.

She sees the strong Penelope. The brave, confident woman I could be if I stopped caring so much about what my mom thinks.

A future with Syn is within my grasp... once I tell Mom to go fly a kite.

"Mmm." Syn rolls to face me, draping an arm over my waist and a leg over mine, trapping me in her heat and burning up my anxious thoughts. She's the remedy I never knew existed, and I never want to let her go.

"Good morning," I whisper, kissing her jaw.

When I pull back, she smiles and taps my temple. "It's too early to be thinking so loud. What's going on up here?"

"You're right."

She hums. "Usually am."

Laughing, I bury my face against her neck. "I think I'm pansexual. How big of an aneurism do you think my mom will have when she finds out?" As much as I want to disappear into Syn's embrace, I pull back and meet her eyes.

"Does it matter?"

Words evade me, and I bite my lip.

"You're happy, right?"

Lump in my throat, I nod.

"And I treat you right?"

"Better than anyone."

Her finger glides along my cheek. "That's all that matters. And when the time comes to tell her, I'll be right there, by your side. I won't let her bully you or belittle you, Penelope. This is the real deal for me, and I won't let her hurt you anymore."

Tears prickle my lashes. "I know, but I'm scared."

Syn swipes the traitorous moisture from my eyes before dropping her lips to my forehead. "I know. And I won't promise you that everything will be okay, because your mom is a judgmental cunt. But I will promise you that, no matter what happens, I'll be there to pick up the pieces."

A soft "okay" is all I can manage as I wind my arms around her waist and soak up her words like a parched sponge.

She'll be there for me.

She cares about me.

"It's Sunday. Should we go to the farmers' market?"

"Mmm." I hug her tighter before leaning back and pushing the rogue strand of violet away from her face.

"Not yet. I'm not done basking in how cute you are the morning after."

Syn's lips purse and pull to the side. "I don't think anyone has ever called me cute before." She hems and haws for a second before adding, "I don't hate it. Do it again."

A giggle bursts from my mouth when I peck her cheek, but I oblige. "You're cute."

Her answering smile is blinding. It exudes unfettered joy, instead of her usual sultriness. It looks good on her.

"Do you know what I thought when we met?" I ask, smoothing a chunk of hair that's sticking out from the side of her head.

Dark eyebrows crinkle. "What?"

My fingers drag down to the toned shoulder muscles that cap her arms. "How beautiful your arms were. I was so nervous that I didn't tell you."

"Do you know what I noticed about you?" Her fingers skate through the ends of my hair.

"How pathetic I was for going on a date with that jerk?"

Dropping my hair, she taps the tip of my nose. "None of that. You're a strong, powerful woman, Penelope Martin."

The more she says it, the more I'm starting to believe it.

"I noticed all this beautiful blonde hair. It reminded me of shimmering threads of gold."

The corners of my mouth twitch with a forced smile. My eyes drop to the aforementioned strands, and loathing fills my gut. "I hate my hair."

Sad eyes meet mine when I find the courage to look at Syn. "Why?"

I shrug. "It's a permanent reminder of her and how she controlled me."

Syn tugs the ends of my hair. "Then cut it."

"I can't."

"Yes. You can, sweetness. You are your own person. Powerful. Strong. *Sexy*. Remember?"

Swallowing the emotion clogging my throat, I nod. I've made so many appointments over the last few years, once I lived on my own and didn't rely on my parents for money. In the end, I chickened out every time. Opting for my usual subtle highlights and a trim.

I would never hear the end of it. How I'd look manly or ugly. How *"women have long hair."*

"Anyway"—I change the subject—"I feel horrible about how badly things went with your sister the other day."

Syn sighs and flops onto her back, but I cuddle against her side. "She'll come around when she realizes how much I care about you." She kisses the top of my head.

Quietness falls between us, and I hope I didn't ruin everything. Instead, I trace the hellhound tattooed on Syn's ribs. Flames rise along its back, its jaw is open on a ferocious growl. "This is beautiful. *Dark*, but beautiful."

Syn's eyes dip down to her side, and her fingers chase after mine. "Lucie did it."

My eyebrows drop. "Really?"

"Mhm. Besides running Hell, art is her passion." She chuckles. "When I was a teen, I would sneak into her studio and watch her paint and draw for hours. She'd get so engrossed in her work; it was like the outside world simply ceased to exist. She had a way of turning the most macabre images into something beautiful."

"Did she know you were there?"

Syn smiles. "Oh, yeah. But I don't think she cared. It was when I felt closest to her, like she was showing me a piece of herself no one else got to see. She did this tattoo when I turned eighteen." Clearing her throat, she shakes her head. "That was before..."

I prop myself onto my elbow. "Before what?"

Syn's fingers curl into the sheets at her waist. "Before Dad was murdered. Before Lucie had to decide whether to fill his shoes or let Hell fall into the wrong hands. She chose the former, which meant she didn't have time for frivolous things like painting and tattooing."

An idea sparks to life in my brain. Lucie is an artist and she knows how to tattoo...

"What if you asked Lucie to partner with you on the new tattoo shop?" I blurt.

Syn's eyebrows crinkle, then rise. "That's actually a pretty genius idea, sweetness."

I brush a hand over my shoulder and puff out my chest. "I have my moments."

"Art was her passion. There's no way she doesn't miss it. I'll text her and see if she can come to the closing this week." Syn reaches over to the nightstand for her phone.

I grab her free arm. "Wait, the Devil has a cell phone?"

"Yeah, I mean, how else am I supposed to communicate with her? Fire and brimstone? Don't be ridiculous." She chuckles before sitting up. "Come on. I bet Fen is starving, and I could go for a Cream Me Up cinnamon roll."

Chapter 19

Synthea

"Sign here." Antoinette's claw hovers over the signature line.

I grab the pen and scribble my name.

"And here." She points to another line on a different page.

Another scratch of the pen.

"And… that's it." Sharp fangs peek out when she smiles.

"That's it?"

"Except for these." Penelope extends her hand, a set of keys dangling from her slim fingers.

After we started dating—at least that's what she calls it; I prefer simply calling her *mine*—we opted to bring

Antoinette in as the primary agent to avoid any conflict of interest. But I wanted my sweetness to get her moment in the spotlight, and all the credit, since she did all the work. Hence, her being here to hand over the coveted keys to my new kingdom.

Twin dimples greet me when she smiles. "Congratulations, Syn."

Grabbing the keys, I pull her in for a hug. My mouth lands on hers, not giving a flying fuck her boss is watching.

A throat clearing has me pulling back… reluctantly. "I'll get all the paperwork finalized, but congratulations on your new property. I can't wait to see what you do with it." Antoinette sweeps the signed papers into her briefcase before slipping out the front door with a final wave.

I spin in a slow circle, taking in the nearly empty storefront. Besides the lonely reception desk next to me, the space is devoid of any furniture—or character. And it's too bright. White walls tower around us, waiting to be filled with moody colors and amazing artwork.

"Do you think she'll show?" Penelope wraps her arms around my waist.

Not unlike her, Lucie didn't dignify me with a response when I texted that I had a proposition for her. I rub a circle on Penelope's lower back. "She has the address. The ball is in her court now."

"What if she says no?"

I shrug. "Her loss."

Pen opens her mouth, but whatever she's going to say is interrupted by a soul-shaking crack of thunder. Her nose crinkles as the distinct sulfuric scent permeates the small shop.

"What's so important?" Irritation ripples through my sister's voice when she materializes in front of us, the flames around her dissipating into a cloud of smoke.

Pen coughs, waving the thick plume away with her hand.

"Hello to you, too, dear sister." I don't hide the sarcasm from my tone, stepping in front of Pen to shield her in case Lucie is in a mood.

Lucie crosses her arms over her chest and juts her hip to the side. "You said you had something important to discuss."

"Yes." I blow out a breath. *Be the bigger demon, Syn. Make things right.* "First, I'm sorry about how things ended last time. I don't like when we fight, Lucie." I'm surprised to find my guilt mirrored in her eyes when they meet mine.

Despite the padded points on the shoulders of her leather jacket, her body deflates in defeat. "Me, too. I let my jealousy get the better of me."

My eyes widen. "Jealousy?"

Lucie nods.

"Of me?"

"After Dad died, the weight of the world was tossed onto my shoulders. No one else was coming to rescue us, so I sacrificed my life to pick up the pieces."

I reach for her, hand falling limp to my side at the last second. "Lucie, I had no idea."

"Why would you? I shut you out after he died. And when you said you wanted to leave Hell... I couldn't ask you to give up your dreams, Syn. Mine were already dead and buried; I couldn't let you sacrifice yours, too."

My ears must be playing tricks on me, but it's my sweetness who voices the question bouncing around my brain. "You mean, you don't want to be Queen?"

I expect Lucie to snap at Pen, like last time, but even the Devil is full of surprises, I guess.

Lucie's glossy, red-stained lips roll inward, and she shakes her head. "I don't know anymore. But do you know what hurts the most?"

I take a step toward her. "What?"

She sniffles. In all my years, I don't think I've ever witnessed this much emotion from my sister. Was she really pushing everything down to protect me?

"I gave up everything for him, and he never even said he was proud of me. Not once. But he adored you, Syn."

My eyes prickle. "He loved you, too, Lucie."

She shakes her head again. "I was a pawn. Emotionless and obedient. A soldier he groomed to someday replace him. You were his child."

"Then do this with me, Sister." I close the distance between us and link my fingers with hers. "I remember your paintings, Lucie. Your art. I still wear it on my skin." I lift my shirt until the golden hellhound on my side dances in the sun. "It's not too late to live your dream. Hell is back under control, and I'm sure Eleazer can handle things for a bit."

Squeezing my hand, Lucie's eyes scan the empty space. "What's your plan, Little Sister?"

I smirk. "A tattoo shop. What do you say? Business partners?"

Lucie's dark gaze slices to Penelope. "This was your idea, wasn't it?" Her tone may be sharp and void of emotion, but a smile plays on the corners of her lips.

Taking a step closer, Pen shrugs. "My brother is one of the most important people to me, so I couldn't stand the thought of Syn not having her sister."

Lucie nods. "I'm sorry for the way I treated you during our first meeting."

Pen's mouth gapes before she slams it shut and mumbles, "It's okay."

"It's really not. How about a do-over?"

My gut clenches as my sister steps in front of my mate and extends a hand.

"I'm Lucie. It's a pleasure to meet my sister's partner."

I'm reminded why I love this human so much when, without hesitation, she grips Lucie's hand. "It's nice to meet you, Lucie. I'm Penelope."

"I think we're going to be great friends." The wicked smirk Lucie flashes my way has me questioning this whole situation. The only demon who'll be corrupting my sweet little human is me.

Pushing between them, I wrap my arms around Pen's waist. "Okay, okay. That's enough."

"Oh! Possessive. You must really like her." Lucie flashes me a wink.

I glance down at Penelope, who's smiling up at me. *You have no idea.*

The bell above the front door jingles, and every head in the place turns to find a pixie with glittering navy wings. "Yo, boss! This place is rad!" Rafe swaggers across the room and tips his head toward Lucie. "Who's the hottie?"

Oof. Open mouth, insert foot.

The air around Lucie crackles, and she scoffs. "You couldn't handle me, twinkletoes."

Never one to back down from a challenge, Rafe's eyes darken as they take a leisurely perusal of Lucie. "Is that a dare, Cruella?"

"Do you know who I am, little boy?" Lucie sneers down her nose at him.

Mouth splitting into a self-assured grin, the cocky fucker says, "No, but you'd look pretty…"

Pen's lips press against my cheek before she murmurs, "I've gotta go. See you later."

She's up to something. My sweetness. She's been a ball of nerves all morning, and it wasn't from the closing.

Before I can chase after her, there's a pained groan behind me.

When I snap my head toward my sister and Rafe, he's clutching his stomach, and she's dusting the spikes that line the shoulders of her jacket.

Ugh, I'm regretting my decision to bring Lucie into this already. She doesn't play well with others. Side effect of being the Queen of Hell.

"Children, please!" I raise my hands in hopes of grabbing their attention.

It works, as two sets of eyes swing to me. One the color of lapis lazuli and laced with smugness. The other, a starless sky, burning with the fury of a thousand suns.

"We're all adults here," I reprimand.

"Some more than others." Lucie crosses her arms over her chest, and Rafe's eyes linger on the way the movement has her tits straining the zipper of her jacket. The dirty dog has the gall to lick his lips.

I shake my head. It's going to be a long day. Swiping my tablet from the reception counter, I pull up my mood board for the shop. "Knock it off, Rafe."

Lucie snickers, and I shoot her a glare. "You, too, Luce. You're not the Devil when you're here. Got it?"

“Got it,” she mumbles, eyes falling to the floor.

“Good. Now, we have work to do.”

CHAPTER 20

I felt bad about leaving Syn to deal with her sister and Rafe. Animosity clogged my breath as soon as Lucie laid eyes on the cocky pixie. I'd be surprised if she doesn't kill him, or at least clip his wings, by the end of the day.

But Syn is strong. She can handle them. She's been doing so for decades—centuries in Lucie's case.

I have something more important to take care of. Something to prove to myself. That deep within me, a strength exists. One that Syn sees.

Since taking the leap from friends to more, that inner strength is bubbling just beneath the surface, and it's time to use it.

“I can’t believe I’m doing this.” Stopping on the top step, I close my eyes and blow out a breath.

My fingers slip into the pocket of my trousers. The sticky note crinkles between them as I pull it free.

I run my thumb over Syn’s familiar handwriting scribbled on the purple paper. The words have my shoulders rolling back and my chin rising. *It’s time to take control, Pen. No more chickening out.* “It’s *my* life, not hers.”

Further inflating my balloon of courage, Syn’s voice echoes in my head. *You are your own person. Powerful. Strong. Sexy.*

I hold my head higher. “Yes, I am.”

After my little pep talk, I push open the door and am greeted by the trickling of water and the twittering of songbirds. Humidity dampens my skin and fills my lungs when I inhale.

Even after a stressful day, one step into Urban Oasis and it all melts away. Nestled inside an old cathedral, Vanessa really knew what she was doing when she designed her spa.

Rainbows scatter around me as sunshine filters through the stained-glass windows. My heels click on the cobblestone path as I approach the reception desk. Vibrant cobalt and amethyst blooms climb the front of the wood, while a small waterfall sits behind it.

Ding! I slap the bell and wait for the receptionist.

A cloud of white hair, burgundy eyes, and pale skin has me sucking in a gasp. "Vanessa!" I pull my friend in for a hug when she comes around the desk. Eucalyptus surrounds me, tamping down the butterflies in my tummy. "I didn't know you were here today."

Fangs poke into her bottom lip when she smiles. "Melody is on vacation, so I'm filling in for the week."

"Did you leave Luc in Maple Ridge Hollow?"

The smile drops from her face at the mention of her grumpy minotaur mate. "Unfortunately. Maggie is gearing up for harvest season, so she needs him more." Vanessa's sister-in-law runs an apple orchard, and Luc is the foreman.

"Poor guy."

Her delicate shoulder shrugs. "Absence makes the heart grow fonder." She winks before heading to the computer nestled amongst the greenery in the reception area. "What brings you in today?"

The reminder of my appointment has my tummy somersaulting again, nerves roaring back to life. "I have an appointment with Ryssa."

"She's running a few minutes behind, but she should be right out. Anyway, how are things going?" She waggles her dark-blonde eyebrows. "I haven't seen you since our girls' trip."

I wring my hands in front of me. "Yeah, about that... Sorry for leaving early."

Ness chuckles. "Well, you're glowing, so things must have worked out with your friend."

My traitorous cheeks heat, scorching my palm when I cup my face. "Yeah." I clear my throat, but my voice still cracks. "It's been really good. Amazing, actually."

"I'm happy for you, Pen. You deserve to be with someone who makes you glow."

Lips spreading into a grin, her words sink in.

"I do, don't I?"

Vanessa smiles. "You do."

The click of hooves behind me interrupts our conversation before it can go any further. A warm arm wraps around my waist, tugging me into a side hug. "Penelope!" Ryssa looks down on me with bright-green doe eyes that match the color of her hair.

"Hi, Ryssa. How are you?"

She slips her hand into mine, pulling me down the path toward the salon area of the spa. A set of small antlers curves away from her face, and her deer-like ears twitch as we walk. "I'm good. I was surprised to see your name on the schedule. It's only been, what, a month since your last appointment?"

My heart hammers as we approach the salon chair, and I take a seat. "It's time for a change."

The black cape whooshes through the air as Ryssa unfurls it, wrapping the material around my body. She braces her hands on my shoulders and meets my gaze in the mirror. "I'm always up for a change. What did you have in mind?"

Mouth dry as a desert, I swallow.

This is it.

My hands curl around the stiff fabric of the cape.

Do it, Penelope.

Do it!

I blow out a breath. "Chop it off."

Ryssa combs her fingers through the end of my ponytail. "Really?"

Gulping, I nod.

Do not chicken out!

Ryssa's answering smile settles my nerves. "It's going to look amazing with your cheekbones and dimples." She picks up a pair of scissors. "Ready?"

As I'll ever be. Exhilaration overthrows the anxiety as the first strand of gold slips between the sleek blades, and I can't help but smile. "Let's do it."

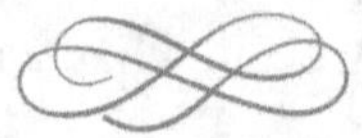

"What do you think?" Ryssa spins me to face the mirror.

Tears spring to my eyes as I run my hands through the short strands.

"Oh, no... Please, don't cry, Pen. I-I can fix it. We can add some extensions. No one will ever know."

Laughter bubbles from my throat as salty drops wet my flushed cheeks. "I love it, Ryssa."

"You do?"

I fluff the top before tucking a chunk behind my ear. "I do." Staring back at me in the mirror is the woman I'm meant to be. Hair shorn short on the sides but longer on top; when I smile, my dimples pop like never before. Ryssa was right. My skin may be blotchy and red from crying, but I've never been happier. This is who I should have been all along. "I finally look like me." My eyes swing to her reflection. "Thank you."

Her hand lands on my shoulder, and she squeezes, face splitting into a smile that rivals mine. "You look beautiful, Pen. Thank you for trusting me with such a big transformation."

Ryssa finishes cleaning up while I play with my new pixie cut. Excitement simmers beneath my skin. I can't wait to show Syn.

After paying—and leaving a large tip—I trade the tranquility of the spa for the hustle and bustle of the New York City sidewalk. The entire walk to the Taproom, my eyes are glued to my reflection in every storefront I pass. A weight I didn't realize I'd been bogged down by for years is finally gone, and I can't wipe the smile off my face.

It's firmly in place when I grip the familiar S-shaped handle and enter the Taproom.

On autopilot, my feet carry me to the bar in search of my purple-haired demon. Instead, my hot-air balloon of adrenaline deflates a little when I find a tattooed pixie instead.

From behind the bar, Rafe's eyes grow to a comical size. He brings his fingers to his mouth, a wolf whistle following when he puffs his cheeks and blows. "Looking good, Pen."

It's all in good fun, but the catcall has my shoulders rolling back as I run a hand over the back of my hair. "Thanks. Have you seen, Syn?"

He hooks a thumb over his shoulder toward the hallway that leads to Syn's office. "Paperwork."

"Thank you." One final wave and I head to the small office at the end of the hall.

Rather than knocking, I crack the door and poke my head inside. Elbow propped on her desk, Syn's chin rests on her hand. Her eyes track something on the computer screen, and her dark eyebrows scrunch.

"You look busy," I say, slipping into the room and closing the door. "Maybe I should come back later."

Head swiveling toward me, her lips curl into the sultry grin that I love so much. She unfolds her body from the chair and stalks toward me with predatory steps. "For you, sweetness, I'm never too busy."

Syn towers over me, so I'm forced to tip my head back to maintain eye contact. "How did things go with Lucie and Rafe? He's still alive, so I assume that's a good sign."

One hand braced on the door, she leans in and runs her nose along my jaw, forcing a shiver down my spine. "We're not going to talk about them right now," she purrs in my ear.

I tilt my head to the side, barely swallowing my moan when she nips my earlobe. "W-We're not?"

Pulling back, Syn shakes her head. Her free hand wraps around my neck, holding me hostage. "Nah, sweetness. We're gonna talk about you."

"Me?" I play dumb, allowing the sexual tension between us to flourish.

Her lips hover over mine. "Yes. I want to talk about this haircut that you snuck off to get."

I wince, eyes dropping to the floor. "I was going to—"

Her fingers tightening around my throat halt my words.

"Do you know how much you're glowing right now? Seeing you embrace who you're meant to be and not the construct your mother created. It's... *sexy*."

My gaze springs back to hers, which is simmering with desire. "Sexy?"

"Yeah, and I need a taste." Releasing my throat, her hand runs down the front of my body to the button on my pants. She pops it open and lowers the zipper. "So how about you take these pants off and get your fine ass on my desk so I can show you how sexy you are?"

Coming from anyone else, such crass and blatantly sexual language would turn me into a flustered mess. With Syn, I crave her words. My body lights up when she calls me a good girl or reminds me that I am a sexual creature.

Head held high, I cross the room to her desk and slip off my heels and slacks.

Besides my labored breaths and the click of a lock sliding into place, the room is silent, the air thick with yearning and the promise of pleasure. It's almost too much to bear.

A presence at my back and hot breaths against the side of my neck have my hands lingering on the waistband of my panties. "Leave those on... for now." A dark vow laces the smooth honey of her voice, ramping up the anticipation rushing through my veins.

"Should we really be doing this here? At your job?" Pressure on my lower back has me tipping forward, hands slapping onto the top of Syn's desk.

Something warm slithers around my waist and into the front of my underwear. "Don't worry, sweetness. I locked the door. No one will bother us."

I suck in a gasp as the thing in my panties nestles against my clit and rumbles to life. *Her tail.* This time, I can't stop my moan from breaking free. My head hangs between my arms as I rock my hips and ride a tidal wave of bliss.

"Do you know how strong you are, Penelope?" Warmth blankets my back as Syn's fingers curl around the edge of the desk, bracketing my hips. "I'm proud of you for taking control of your life. It's unbelievably sexy."

Arousal trickles from my opening, wetting my underwear when the tip of her tail circles my clit. "Mhmm, that feels good."

"Yeah? How about you tell me what you want me to do?"

Ice water douses the flames in my core, freezing me in place. "What? I-I can't." My voice wobbles.

Syn grips my chin, twisting my head until I meet her gaze. "Yes. You can. You're a strong, powerful, confident woman. Tell me what you want, Pen."

Knocking her hand away from my jaw, I spin within the cage of her arms. Her tail slips away from my core, and my butt collides with the edge of the desk when I raise my chin. "Get on your knees." The command is shaky. "A-And eat my cunt." The words roll off my tongue easier than I anticipated. And they feel... *good*. Amazing, actually.

Dark horns gleam under the fluorescent lights as she drops to her knees. A feral grin seizes my demon's beautiful face, transforming her into the Hell-born princess she is. "That's my girl."

Triggered by her praise, my back arches, and my fingers curl around the thick base of her horns. The rough keratin against my palms pulses in time with her heartbeat, the rapid rhythm proving she's just as turned on as I am.

Hot puffs of air ghost up my thighs before Syn drags her nose over the sopping lace covering my center. "Do you know how good you smell?" Her hands wrap around my waist, boosting me onto her desk.

Shaking my head, my legs spread to accommodate her body. "T-Tell me." I clear my throat. "Tell me what I do to you."

Where is this confidence coming from?

Syn groans, gripping the sides of my panties. There's a sharp snap of pressure against my hips, then *rrrrip,* blue lace flutters to the floor. "So sweet." Her tongue drags through the wetness seeping out of me, and she moans. "Like the most decadent dessert. One I want to devour until I can't possibly eat another bite. You've got me all twisted in knots, sweetness. Don't you see it?"

An emotion swims to the surface of her dark eyes. One that has my heart ready to explode out of my chest.

One I've never felt with this level of urgency.

One I'm not sure I'm ready to face.

So I bury my head in the sand, using my grip on her horns to bury Syn's face between my thighs.

She goes willingly, lips suctioning to my opening while her tongue dives deep inside.

A wave of pleasure surges through me, curling my body forward. "Oh," I moan. "More." *So much more.*

Syn's fingers leave divots on my thighs as she spreads me wider and shuffles closer, her mouth never leaving my core and inching me closer to the inevitable peak. I welcome it, waiting with bated breath to be shoved over the cliff.

My hand slips from her horn, instead sifting through her chin length messy purple mane. "Please, don't stop. I'm so close."

The subtle buzz of her tail breaks through my lust-filled brain. Its tip lands on my clit again, igniting fireworks under my skin. Eyes slamming shut, I tip my head back and bite my lip to stifle my cry as I'm swept into a tsunami of euphoria.

Crashing waves ebb to a gentle lapping at the shore. Sawing breaths slow to a gentle pant.

Head tipping down, my eyes open to find a very smug demon licking her lips. "You good, sweetness?"

Clear fluid coats her mouth and chin. The sight should repulse me and have my cheeks heating with embarrassment. In another life, it would have, but not now. Not with Syn at my feet.

Instead, I find an untamable urge barreling through me. The need to taste and claim forces my body from the desk.

In the blink of an eye, I tackle Syn. She falls onto her butt with an *oomph.* I grip the sides of her face and smash my mouth to hers. Sweet and tangy, my tongue chases the flavor. *My* flavor. And I can't get enough.

"We're just getting started," Syn mumbles between sloppy kisses. "Hang on tight."

On instinct, I obey, wrapping my arms around her neck while attacking her mouth and jaw with mine.

Thunder claps, heat surrounds us, then everything goes black. A split second later, Syn's room materializes, and we bounce onto the bed in a tangle of limbs.

Chapter 21

Penelope

"What was that?" I press a hand to Syn's shoulder, but it doesn't stop her from kissing a path down the side of my throat.

My head is dizzy, but I'm not sure if it's from arousal or what just happened.

"Teleporting." The word is muffled against my skin. "Needed you in my bed." She tugs my blouse over my head, continuing to nip and suck her way down my body.

"You can teleport?" I grip her hair and force her to look at me.

A long black nail circles my belly button. Syn shrugs and licks her lips. “It’s not a big deal. That’s how I got to your place so fast the night you got evicted.”

“A little warning next time, maybe?” I cock my eyebrow at her, but the drag of her fingers across my stomach has my brain turning to mush.

“Sorry,” she says, but I doubt she means it because she rolls on top of me and pins my wrists to the bed. “Heat of the moment. Now, where were we?”

Nestled between my legs, she grinds her hips down. The stiff denim of her jeans drags against my clit. Arousal blooms in my naked core, and I moan.

“I already ate your pretty cunt, so what’s next?” She leans down, purring the words into my ear.

Lust acts as a shield of bravery, and I say, “You could fuck me.”

“I like the way you think, sweetness.” A dark shadow unfurls from her body, slithering between my back and the mattress.

I arch to give it more room.

The band on my bra pulls tight before loosening, the lace cups tugged away from my breasts by one of Syn’s long nails.

Suddenly, I’m aware that I’m completely naked while she’s fully clothed. A rush of warmth spreads through me, coloring my skin a soft pink. No matter how many times she’s seen me naked, my stomach still ties itself into a knot.

Syn sits back on her knees and grips my waist. In a slow perusal, her eyes caress my body before rising to my face. "You're beautiful, Penelope."

Poof! Like some sort of magic potion, her compliment unties the pretzel my stomach was wrapped in, and my nerves settle. "I'd feel better if you were naked, too," I say as I slip my hands under her shirt.

She chuckles, but strips out of her clothes.

I can't help but marvel as, sliver by sliver, all of her gray skin is exposed. Golden ink shimmers in intricate designs on her arms, chest, and ribs. My fingers twitch with the need to trace each line and flourish like my very own treasure map.

I don't think I'll ever get tired of looking at her.

Touching her.

Existing beside her.

Is this what real love feels like?

Unconditional. Raw.

Not bound by arbitrary standards set by someone else.

Oxygen stalls in my lungs as my eyes burn. Syn grips my chin, drawing my gaze to hers. "What's wrong?"

Blood pounds in my ears. "I think I love you."

Why did I say that?

Stupid, Penelope.

You just ruined everything. It's too soon. She's going to kick you out. You'll be homeless and alone and—

Her lips find mine, soft yet demanding. "I think I love you, too, sweetness."

My breath catches. "Really? Are you sure?"

She nods, mouth dragging against mine. "How could I not?"

I giggle, but it turns into a moan when she nips my lower lip with her sharp teeth.

"Now that that's out of the way, I owe you a good fucking." Fingers wrapped around my waist, Syn rolls onto her back, leaving me straddling her hips.

I gasp at the sudden reversal of our positions. "What are you—"

"I want you to be in charge right now, sweetness. Show me how strong and confident you are." Two shadows wrap around her body. They weave themselves together into a phallic shape that juts out from Syn's pelvis. It's thick and girthy—and intimidating. "You think you can take all of me, baby girl?"

I gulp. Hands braced on her abdomen, I stare down at the new appendage. I don't think I've ever put something *that* big inside me. "Ummm."

Her hand cups my jaw to lift my eyes to hers. "It'll fit. And it'll feel good. I promise."

"Do I just—" My hand shakes as I grip the base. Surprisingly, the shadows are soft to the touch. They're also coated in a thin sheen, making them slippery.

Syn's hand wraps around mine, giving me the confidence to rise onto my knees.

The tip slips inside and stretches me as I slide down.

"Good girl," Syn praises, her hands gripping my hips as I take another inch. "How does it feel?"

Tingles spread from my core to the rest of my body, followed by a warming sensation. I tip my head down and moan. "Mmm... Warm. Tingly. So good."

Her chuckle jostles me another inch down the shadow phallus. "That's the aphrodisiac fluid entering your system through your cunt. It will heighten your orgasm."

Held hostage by my pleasure, all I can do is nod and rock my hips, taking the rest of her inside me. Wetness coats my inner thighs. I bite my lower lip, whimpering when the head of her tail nestles against my clit. I know the vibrations are coming. I crave that sensation, and the anticipation is killing me.

"What do you need, sweetness? I want to hear you say it."

I jolt when her tail slaps against my clit. Pleasure zips through me, and I fall forward. My hands land on either side of Syn's neck, bringing us face to face. I meet the hazy lust in her eyes and say, "The vibrations. Please." Rocking my hips, I sandwich her tail between us and chase the friction I so desperately need.

"Is this what you need?" Her tail roars to life, wedged between our clits. Dark eyes roll into the back of her head, and her sharp teeth sink into her lower lip, like she's fighting to keep composure.

On a cry of pleasure, I tip my head back as the vibrations surge through me. Hips writhing, I ride my pretty demon until I think I might spontaneously combust.

Lost in my own world, I barely notice when something slippery glides down the valley of my ass, nudging at my back entrance.

"Do you remember what I said that first night?" Syn's voice drips with carnal need.

I shake my head, which is too fuzzy to remember anything. All I can do is be in this moment and let the pleasure consume me.

The blunt tip of the shadow teases my puckered hole. For reasons I don't quite understand, my hips push back, seeking the added pressure.

"I want to fill all your holes, sweetness. Every. Single. One." A third shadow slithers over my shoulder before wrapping around my neck, the end coming up to rest at the corner of my mouth. "I bet you'd look so pretty stuffed with me."

Another nudge between my ass cheeks has my core clamping. Adrenaline sends my heart into a frenzy.

Why do I want what she's offering so badly?

Not second guessing myself, I blurt, "Do it."

At a snail's pace, the slick tip between my cheeks ventures forward, breaching the tight muscle. The slight burn and uncomfortableness is soothed when Syn's tail vibrates faster against my clit.

After a few testing thrusts, we settle into a rhythm that has me moaning. I rise and fall on the shadows in my pussy, while Syn impales me from behind with the other shadow.

"You good, sweetness?"

My eyes roll. I'm so full, I think I might burst, but it's amazing. "Don't stop," I pant.

Burning me slowly from the inside out, my orgasm ignites.

Is this what I've been missing my entire adult life? Who knew sex could be this good?

"Ready for one more?"

My head swings up and down as the shadow creeps toward my mouth. I open willingly, knowing this will push me over the edge. The dark tendril slips against my tongue with ease, nudging the back of my throat and bringing tears to my eyes.

I gag, muscles constricting in my throat, but my hips continue their quest toward my peak as the fire rages in my core.

Syn pulls the shadow free, and I gasp, lungs on fire as I suck in a breath. "Again. Please."

"Tap my shoulder if it's too much. Okay?" Our gazes meet, hers brimming with concern.

I nod. "Okay."

“Good girl.” The praise sends a ripple down my spine, and Syn groans when my core clenches.

Can she feel…?

I contract my inner muscles again. A hoarse cry rips from her throat.

Well, that’s a curious development.

Before I can experiment more, the spit-slicked shadow forces its way past my lips once more. I focus on breathing through my nose as Syn pummels my throat and ass.

Grunting, her fingers dig into my hips, and she thrusts into me from below.

Sloppy, wet slurping and gagging fill my ears. A few months ago, the sounds would have disgusted me.

Not anymore. Now, the pornographic symphony has me on the verge of exploding.

I moan around the shadow in my mouth, lips stretched wide, the corners burning as my vision blurs.

In this moment, all I want is to give myself over to euphoria.

So I do.

I focus on the vibrations against my clit. The slick slide of my pussy with each roll of my hips. The squelch of the shadow taking me from behind. And finally, the shadow stalled in my throat, forcing tears and saliva to drip down my face. The combination slingshots me into oblivion, darkness taking over my senses until I’m floating.

The embodiment of bliss.

I never want it to end.

It does, of course. All too soon.

My eyes flutter open, and I'm lying next to Syn. Her fingers stroke hair away from my sweaty brow. "There you are." She smiles, kissing my cheek. "How do you feel?"

A dopey grin pulls up the corners of my lips. "That was amazing." The smile drops from my face when I realize... "What about you? Did you come?"

She cups my face and chuckles. "Yeah, sweetness. I did."

Every ounce of energy is zapped from my body, and I'm left a sated mess. I snuggle into Syn's side, not caring that we should probably shower and change the sheets. It can wait until later. "Can you feel what your shadows feel?"

The scrape of her fingers against my scalp has my eyes drooping. "They're part of me. Like an arm or a leg. So, yeah, I feel what they feel."

"So you could feel it when I squeezed—"

Syn snorts. "Yes, Pen, I could feel your cunt and your ass strangling me. And it was the best thing I've ever felt. We *will* be doing that again."

Giving up the fight, my eyes shut. I roll onto my side, draping an arm over Syn's waist and burying my nose in her neck. "Good. Because I think I liked it."

Last night was... *Wow*. There are no words. Who knew all holes filled was my thing? But apparently, it is. New kink unlocked.

Syn woke me after I napped for an hour and made me drink an entire bottle of water followed by eating some leftover chicken fried rice. "You're probably dehydrated, and I don't want a blood sugar crash triggering a migraine," she said while feeding me a forkful of food.

Even now, her thoughtfulness has my insides liquifying.

I loop one lace under the other and pull tight, tying a neat bow on my sneaker. Next to the couch, Fen paces, drool dripping from around the fluorescent yellow ball in his mouth. "Hold your horses. I'm almost ready."

When I got up to pee, Syn looked so peaceful that I figured I'd let her sleep in and take Fen for his morning romp in the park before work. I should have time to swing by Cream Me Up for some coffee and bagels on the way home, too.

"I like this," I say, shoving my phone into the pocket of my leggings. While I snap my belt bag around my waist, Fen tips his head to the side, listening intently. "Domestic bliss with the woman I love." That four-letter word has my heart swelling.

Fen whines, bumping my leg with his snout and leaving behind a wet nose mark.

"And you, too," I add, scratching behind his ear until his tail beats against the floor. "Come on," I say, grabbing the slobbery ball from his mouth and waving it side to side. "This isn't gonna fetch itself."

Spiked tail swishing behind him, Fen runs the whole way to the park with me hot on his heels. The ache in my thigh muscles has my cheeks heating as memories of last night flash across my eyes.

The whole experience was exhilarating.

I owe it to Syn for awaking this sexual creature inside me. She didn't make me feel ashamed for wanting the things I want or for letting her use me like she wanted.

This early in the morning, the park is deserted except for one or two joggers. Lit by the first inklings of sunrise, I find an empty bench near an open grassy knoll. Fen drops the ball on the ground at my feet. I pick it up and toss it as far as I can.

We fall into a pattern. I throw the ball, and he brings it back. The monotony allows me to get lost in thoughts of what my future would look like with Syn.

No house in the Hamptons. No white picket fence. No two-point-five kids.

Instead, I'd spend my life chasing my dreams alongside Syn. Being unapologetically me and loving unconditionally in a city that's become my home.

Sounds pretty good to me.

A buzzing against my leg rips me from my daydreams. Syn must be awake and missing me. I smile as I tug my phone from my pocket.

The name on the screen has my stomach clenching. With a harsh swallow, I swipe to accept the call and bring the phone to my ear.

"Hi, Mom. You're up early."

Did my voice wobble?

Did she notice?

"Penelope. Labor Day is next weekend."

Oh, fiddlesticks. I've been so caught up in the relationship developing between me and Syn that I completely forgot about Mom expecting me for Labor Day dinner.

What if I tell her I'm sick and can't come this year?

She'd send you on a 300-mile-long guilt trip.

Ignorant of my inner turmoil, Mom continues. "If you don't have a date, I'll invite Josephine's son. He's a nice boy. Single. Looking—"

"I have a date," I blurt, then instantly regret it.

Her voice perks up. "You do? Well, that's wonderful! Do I know him? Where did you meet?"

Him. I run a hand through my hair, tugging at the short strands. "Ummm, it's new."

"It's about time. Your father and I are very excited to meet him. We'll expect you at six for dinner and drinks."

With my tongue stuck to the roof of my mouth, all I can do is nod and hum my agreement.

A large figure in my periphery settles on the bench beside me as Mom says goodbye and hangs up. I'm left reeling.

I'm not ready for her judgement about me and Syn. I want to live in our bubble for a little longer and pretend my mom isn't a colossal narcissist who cares more about appearances than her daughter's happiness.

Guess that was wishful thinking because the other shoe just dropped.

"I almost didn't recognize you." The masculine voice—one I never thought I'd hear again—has my skin prickling and all the hair on my body standing on end.

Slowly, I turn my head. Matthew, the date from hell, has his big body spread out on the bench next to me. "What are you doing here?"

Ignoring my question, he waves a hand at me. "What's with the dyke haircut? Did you switch teams or something?"

The muscles in my jaw jump when I grind my teeth. "Or something." My gaze snaps to the open field across from us, searching for any sign of black fur and glowing red eyes.

Where the hell is Fen? I could use a big, scary hellhound right about now.

"What do you want, Matthew?" I seethe. Come on, Fen. I didn't throw the ball *that* far.

He shrugs, like he wasn't an utter asshole on our date, and I didn't throw my drink on him. "I thought we could catch up. Maybe try again?"

He's up to something.

Keeping one eye on the field, I cock an eyebrow at him. "Really? Did my mother put you up to this?"

A flash of black catches my eye, and I whistle. Fen's ears twitch, and he turns his head my way.

I tip my head toward Matthew and widen my eyes. *Get over here!* I scream internally.

That lights a fire under him, and he breaks into a canter.

Clutching my phone in my hand, I stand, only to be halted by fingers wrapping around my wrist. "I think you owe me after your hissy fit last time." The implication in his tone is clear.

"*Wow*, you're a disgusting excuse for a human." I glare down my nose at him, speaking through gritted teeth. "I don't owe you or anyone else *anything*. Remove your hand. *Now*."

He stands, towering over me in an attempt at intimidation, but I don't cower. "Or what?"

A ferocious growl sounds from my left, and I roll my shoulders back. "Or Fen will take a nice big chunk out of you."

The hair alongside the spikes on Fen's back stands on end. Eyes glowing brighter than normal, his muzzle pulls back to expose a row of vicious teeth, dripping with saliva. Surrounded by flames, he stalks toward Matthew, pouncing at the last second and tackling him to the ground.

Paws braced on Matthew's chest, the enormous hellhound snarls and snaps his jaws an inch from the idiot's face. Matthew trembles and whimpers, a wet patch darkening the fabric of his gray shorts. "I'm sorry. I didn't mean it. I didn't—" He's reduced to a blubbering mess on the ground.

I whistle, and Fen comes to my side, sitting at attention like the good boy he is. Careful to avoid the fire dancing along his shoulders, I stroke a hand through his fur. "I never want to see you again, Matthew."

Scrambling to his feet, tears stream down his face as he nods.

Not so tough now, are you?

Giddiness fills me as he retreats, tail tucked between his legs.

I turn toward Fen, rubbing the sides of his neck with both hands. "Who's the goodest boy?"

He pants, tail whacking the bench.

"I think you earned yourself a cinnamon roll."

Any lingering flames extinguish in a haze of smoke as his eyes close. His chest rumbles with a groan.

The reality of the situation hits me like a ton of bricks as I wrap my arms around his big neck. Things could have turned out so much worse. Shuddering, I banish those thoughts and bury my face in his fur. An inhale of his smoky scent calms my thundering heart. Tears clog my throat as I whisper, "Thank you for protecting me."

Chapter 22

My cupcake is upset. A slight tremble shakes her small body, and her fingers never unclench from the fur on my neck as we leave the park.

It will be okay, cupcake.

I wish the princess would mate with our sweet human already so she could hear me.

The princess. Oh, she will be most unhappy about what that twat did to my cupcake. He got what he deserved. I snicker as my cupcake opens the door to the diner.

My nose goes into overdrive. The distinct scents of sugar, grease, and the dirt water everyone loves to drink in the morning.

Although, I have seen the princess drink it at night, too.

Strange demon. Why would one want to be awake all night when one could be sleeping?

I *love* sleeping. It is one of my favorite activities.

"Hi, Phil." My cupcake greets the big green man behind the counter with a small wave and a smile. She is so sweet.

"Morning, Penelope. What can I get for you and Fen today?" He tips his head to me, and I pull back my upper lip in an attempt at a smile. Laughter booms from his chest.

I guess my smile is not as pretty as my human companion.

As she recites her order to the big green man, I rest my head on the counter, keeping watch for any danger. The diner is nearly empty since it is still early.

A few moments later, my cupcake slides a plate in front of me. "And this is for you, Fen."

Drool pools on my tongue as I am hit by the saccharine scent of the sticky white goo on top. Frosting? Is that what the princess calls it? A wave of cinnamon comes rushing behind. My favorite!

I yip, diving my snout into the warm pastry, devouring half of it in one bite.

A giggle has me turning toward my cupcake. She scratches behind my ears, and I groan. Why does that feel so good?

My tail thumps against the floor as my back foot spasms.

"Good boy," she coos. From anyone else, I would bite their head off for using such words. But my cupcake can do no wrong. Not ever. "Finish your treat so we can get home to Syn." She holds up a pink bag in one hand and a contraption housing two cups in the other.

I scarf down the second half of the scrumptious treat and lick the delightful white frosting from my lips. Belly full, I turn toward my cupcake. "Woof!"

"Ready, boy?" More ear scratches have my eyes rolling and my back leg twitching again.

For the short journey home, I trot alongside my cupcake. No one will hurt her on my watch. Not that scum in the park or anyone else. A growl rumbles from my chest. The man passing us on the sidewalk widens his eyes. He gives us a wide berth when I bare my teeth.

My cupcake is none the wiser, digging in the satchel around her waist for something, when the man scampers away. I huff under my breath.

"Now, listen." Spinning to face me, my cupcake points her key at me before placing it in the doorknob. "I know you can communicate with Syn, like, in her mind or whatever, but *I* will tell her what happened today. Okay?"

Spoilsport. Can a warrior not brag about his conquests in this modern society?

I widen my eyes and whine. This has gotten me many a sweet treat in the past. Surely, it will work on the little human.

She shakes her head. "Uh-ah. Don't give me the puppy eyes, mister. I'm not falling for it."

I whine again.

"I'll make you a deal."

My ears perk up.

"There may or may not be another cinnamon roll in here." Raising a hand, she shakes the pink bag. "It's all yours if you let me handle Syn."

Just the thought of another ooey-gooey cinnamon roll has my tongue escaping my mouth. Drool plops onto the sidewalk.

"Deal?" She extends a hand toward me.

I dip my chin, then place my paw in her palm. Wrapping her fingers around my foot, she gives it a shake.

"Glad we understand each other." She opens the door, ushering me inside with the wave of a hand. "After you."

Chapter 23

Synthea

Yawn ripping from my mouth, I scratch the back of my neck. The apartment door flies open as I walk into the kitchen. Fen trots inside, tongue lolling out the side of his mouth, eyes bright. Penelope enters a second later, with a Cream Me Up bag and cup holder in hand.

The sight of my sweetness has any lingering sleepiness evaporating on the spot.

"How was your walk?" Hooking an arm around her waist, I pull her to me and press my lips to hers. She melts in my embrace and moans softly.

All too soon, she dances out of my arms, sliding the food and drinks onto the kitchen table. "Ummm. About that." She wrings her hands in front of her. "You should probably sit down."

My hand grips the back of the chair, and I arch an eyebrow. "Why?"

Busying her hands, she empties the takeout bag, laying out napkins before placing down two bagels and a cinnamon roll. "Do you remember Matthew?"

I scoff, plopping into my seat and pulling an everything bagel toward me. "How could I forget that colossal waste of space? Misogynistic asshat."

"I sort of ran into him at the park."

I'm out of my chair in the next nanosecond. "What?!"

"It's fine." Penelope raises her hands, as if to calm my heaving chest and racing heart. "He made some rude comments and grabbed my wrist."

"He *touched* you? I'm gonna kill him," I spit. Pain pricks my palms as I fist my hands, nails digging into the skin.

Penelope grabs my wrist. "No, you're not. Fen and I took care of it."

My gaze slices to the hellhound tasked with protecting my sweetness. "How?"

Lifting his head from the cinnamon roll, he licks icing off his snout. "*I did my job,*" he growls in my head. "*I protected my cupcake. The cowardly twat soiled himself.*"

I can't help but laugh. "He pissed himself?"

Pen pats him on the head, smiling down at the beast. "Fen was pretty terrifying." Taking a seat at the table, she pulls on my hand until I sit, too. “Come on. Eat. Drink.” She tips her head to my bagel and the to-go cup that probably contains my favorite drink because my mate is thoughtful like that.

Not your mate.

Not yet.

“I’m sorry for overreacting.” I soften my voice and clutch her hand. “Are you okay? That should’ve been my first concern.”

Pen nods. “I’m fine. I was a little shaken up at first, but I’m okay. I promise.”

“Tell me what happened.”

She blows out a breath that ruffles her hair. “My mom called.”

“Ugh.”

“Yeah. She wanted to make sure I had a date for Labor Day dinner.” She rolls her eyes.

“What did you tell her?”

“I told her I had a date… but…” Her gaze drops to the table. “I didn’t correct her when she assumed it was a man.” Slowly, cerulean irises rise to meet mine, guilt shimmering in the oceanic pools. “Are you mad?” she whispers.

“About what?”

“That I didn’t tell my mom I’m dating a woman. I’m not ready to leave our little bubble yet, Syn. I’m terrified of what she’s going to say and… and I don’t want to lose you because of her.” A tear rolls down her cheek.

"Penelope, sweetness, I'm not going anywhere. If your mother hates that you're in love with a woman, then fuck her."

"I know. She caught me off guard, and I didn't want to deal with a blow-up. Is that bad?"

I squeeze her hand. "No. You're allowed to come out when *you* want. No one should ever force you to out yourself, and it seems like that's what this morning would have been."

She peeks up from beneath wet lashes. "So you're not mad?"

"No. Does this mean I'm your date?" Batting my eyelashes, I fluff my hair and smirk as I wait for her response.

She giggles. "Synthea Hellfyre, would you like to meet my horrific mother and accompany me to the Martin family Labor Day dinner in the Hamptons next weekend?"

"So formal. I wouldn't miss it for the world, sweetness." I wink. "We're in this together... So what does one wear to a Martin family gathering?"

Penelope's laughter has my heart warming. Together, we'll get through whatever hurtful and hateful things her mom says about us, because I have a feeling that woman will never accept her daughter. And I'll be the one gluing Penelope back together after she's shattered by rejection.

Shoulder braced against the doorframe, I observe Penelope in silence. In front of the full-length mirror, she fusses with her hair and smooths her hands down the front of her floral jumpsuit. Her eyes close, throat bobbing with a harsh swallow.

She's nervous.

Which is understandable, considering the hornet's nest that awaits us at her parents' house.

The need to calm her, to soothe her, has me pushing away from my perch and sauntering up behind her.

Warmth simmers under my skin, swallowing my heart when I spot the purple sticky notes lining the frame of the mirror. Reaching over Penelope's shoulder, I pluck one off and smile. "You kept them?"

I skim the messy chicken scratch. This was the first note I left the morning after she moved in.

In the reflection, her eyes flit to mine. "Of course I did." Slender fingers pinch the paper, wiggling it from my grip.

"I drew strength from them when I needed it most." Her gaze turns reverent as she smooths the note back into place.

"Damn, you're amazing... and gorgeous. How did I get so lucky?" I rest my hands on Penelope's hips, admiring the way the floral fabric hugs every dip and curve on her petite body.

As expected, a rosy hue paints her cheeks at my compliment. "I was just thinking the same thing." She spins to face me, fingers plucking at the buttons on my suit vest.

"You like it?" I turn in a slow circle, giving her plenty of time to appreciate the tight hug of the tailored pants on my ass and the sleek vest that leaves my tattooed arms on display. Since she told me how much she loves my arms, I've been making a habit of wearing tank tops and cut-offs. Penelope gets to admire the toned muscles, and I get to soak up her attention. It's a win-win situation for everyone.

My lips curl into a smirk once I face her again, finding hunger looming in her azure gaze. "I just have one question," she says, eyes lingering on my chest.

I prowl forward until her back hits the wall. "Oh?"

Pupils blowing wide, she tips her head back to meet my gaze. A coquettish grin has her dimples popping. "What are you hiding underneath?"

I chuckle. This is good. The playful back-and-forth is distracting her from her nerves. I pop the top button, revealing a hint of black lace.

Penelope licks her lips, eyes glued to my fingers as they work the second button free. "I wish we could just stay home." Her voice shakes, the earlier anxiety returning.

Leaning into her space, I thread my fingers through the back of her hair and bring her attention to my face. "We don't have to go, sweetness. If you're not ready to come out, we can wait."

Eyelids closing, Pen shakes her head. "No, I need to do this. I need to start living the life I want." Fire dances in her eyes when they open again. "And that's with you, Syn. If Mom can't see how unbelievably happy you make me, then maybe it's time to finally cut her out of my life. It's something I should've done a long time ago, but you finally gave me the courage."

"Nah, sweetness, that's all you. My brave, strong, beautiful mate."

She sucks in a breath. "Mate? D-Do you want—"

My forehead finds hers, lips mere centimeters apart. "Yeah, sweetness, I want you to be my mate."

She squeals, throwing herself at me. Catching her, I brace her weight against the wall when she wraps her legs around my waist.

One thumb skating over her cheekbone, my other hand cups her ass. "I was going to wait until after tonight, but no time like the present."

Her fingers curl around the edges of my vest, bringing her chest flush against mine. "Gives me something good to look forward to because I don't think dinner is going to go well."

"I'll be there, however you need me to be, okay?"

She nods.

"If you need me to tell your mom to fuck off, I will. If you need me to hold your hand and keep my mouth shut, I will." I smirk. "I'll hate every second of it, but I'll do it because I love you, Penelope."

My heart sings when her lips brush mine and she says, "I love you, too, Syn."

I'm not sure how long we stand like that, encapsulated in our orb of love and joy, but Penelope eventually breaks it by sighing. "We should probably go soon so we're not late."

Reluctantly, I set her back on her feet and re-button my vest. "Are you sure you don't want to stay the night? It's a long drive—which I certainly don't mind. Two hours of you hugging me tight while we zoom down the highway. Sounds like heaven to me."

Penelope laughs, smacking a kiss on my cheek. "I'm sure I'll be emotionally exhausted, and I'd much rather sleep in my own bed."

Slipping past her, I grab one of my leather jackets from the closet. "You mean *my* bed."

I yelp at a sharp sting on my right ass cheek. *Did she pinch me?*

Sly as a fox, she grins, sidling up next to me. "You mean *our* bed."

"Our bed," I agree. "I like the sound of that."

Reaching past me, she runs her fingers over one of my other jackets. "Quite the collection you have here... Can I borrow one?"

The organ in my chest stops beating. My sweet little human in *my* leather jacket? Sign me the fuck up. "Fuck, yeah." In my haste to grab my favorite from the hanger, I knock a couple of sweaters to the ground.

Penelope giggles, but accepts the extended jacket.

She clutches the leather between her hands, brow creasing when she pulls a small tin from the pocket. "What's this?" The contents rattle when she shakes the metal container.

"Oh, ummm..." I scratch the back of my neck, eyes dropping to the floor.

The distinct click of the tin opening echoes through the silent room. I don't have to look. I already know what's inside. "Syn..." she breathes.

"Today is going to be stressful for you, so I wanted to make sure you're covered. Ya know... just in case." As my gaze rises to hers, my mouth pulls up on one side.

Two little foil pill packets rest on the bottom of the tin amongst a scattering of red pain relievers. "Syn." Moisture swims in her beautiful eyes as they meet mine.

Is she going to think this is an invasion of her privacy? Am I being overbearing?

In the next blink, her body crashes into mine, forcing me to take a stumbled step backward. Her arms latch around my neck in a suffocating grip. "Thank you." Holding me tighter, her lips crush mine in a way that steals my breath. "Thank you. Thank you."

My laughter puffs against her mouth. "You already said that, sweetness."

Breaking the embrace, Pen closes the tin and stuffs it back into the pocket. "I don't think you realize how much this means to me. Yes, I usually have meds on me at all times, but sometimes life happens, and I forget. Thank you for easing some of that stress."

"Loving someone should make their life easier. Not harder." Crisp black leather brushes against my fingertips as I grab the jacket from her and hold it up. Taking the hint, Penelope threads one arm, then the other, into the sleeves.

"Something you've proven time and time again. Thank you." She smiles as she shrugs on the jacket.

The juxtaposition between her floral jumpsuit and the worn black leather is better than I could've imagined. Proof she was made for me.

The only thing that would make it better is if she were wearing nothing but my jacket.

She pushes past me, mischievous eyes meeting mine when she glances over her shoulder on her way out of the bedroom. "Are you done drooling? Or did you need a minute?"

I'm pretty sure my tongue drags across the floor as I follow her. *I'll never be done drooling over you, sweetness.*

Chapter 24

Unfortunately, the two-hour ride to my parents' house passed in the blink of an eye. "Are you sure you didn't teleport us here?" I whine, leading us up the meticulous cobblestone driveway to the front porch.

Syn chuckles and stands behind me as we face the bright yellow front door. Such a cheery, happy color. It should be welcoming. For me, it's anything but. Not with the memories I have of my childhood. A pair of strong arms wraps around my waist, quelling the rush of anxiety. "Trust me, sweetness, I took the scenic route and a few wrong turns just to give you more time."

"It's fine." I blow out a breath, smoothing my sweaty palms against my thighs. "I'm fine."

Syn rests her chin on my shoulder. "Say the word, and we're outta here."

I nod. "Labor Day weekend was always my favorite when I was younger." I lean into the warm presence behind me, absorbing the much-needed strength.

"Why's that?"

A smile graces my face as I relive the memory. "Dad would take the whole weekend off, so Mom was on her best behavior. It was the one time of the year I felt like a normal kid. Playing in the pool with Colin. Dad chasing me down the beach and into the ocean." My voice drops to a whisper. "I didn't have to be perfect. I wasn't under her microscope."

"I'm sorry, Pen."

I turn my head until our gazes collide. "Why? It's not your fault the universe dealt me a terrible mom."

"No, but—"

"Come on. Let's get this over with." I take a step forward, my hand trembling as I reach for the doorbell. At the last second, Syn's fingers entwine with mine and, together, we press the little rectangular button.

Every muscle in my body tightens as the bell echoes inside the house, and we wait. The twinkling blue eyes and dimpled smile I'm met by when the door opens have the tension melting from my body. "Hey, Pen."

I leave the safety of Syn's embrace, only to be bundled against my brother's broad chest. "Hey, Colin."

Pulling back, he braces his hands on my shoulders, gaze landing behind me. "Syn, right? Good to see you again." A sly grin curls the corners of his mouth.

It's just like ripping off a Band-Aid, Penelope. I blow out a breath. If anyone will be accepting of me coming out, it's Colin.

Rolling my shoulders back, I step next to Syn and weave my fingers through hers again. "Syn is my girlfriend."

Somehow, his smile widens, those twin dimples popping. I'm pulled in for another hug, but this time Syn comes with. "I'm proud of you, Pen," Colin says against my hair. "By the way, I like the new haircut. It suits you."

I smile, squeezing them tighter, holding on to this moment before it inevitably comes crashing down the second I see Mom.

Colin steps back, and Syn and I follow him into the house. "You're just in time for dinner. Everyone's out back by the pool."

We make our way through the house and out into the backyard. The golden rays of the evening sun reflect off the surface of the pool where my niece and nephew dangle their feet into the water. It's surrounded by a large cement patio that takes up most of the yard.

Manicured to perfection, a paver path leads to a pristine white fence. Beyond the barrier is where I would escape to on my worst days. On the days Mom's barbed words were too much, I'd flee to the sandy shores, wasting hours watching the waves.

Maybe no one will notice if I slip through the gate now...

"Lucky Penny." The baritone of my dad's voice draws me back to the present.

He pulls me in for a quick side hug, never one for overt displays of affection. "Hi, Dad."

His gray eyebrows dip, blue eyes assessing Syn where she stands at my side. "Who's your friend?"

Fingers twisting in the fabric of my jumpsuit, I gulp, but Syn answers before I can. Extending a hand to my dad, she says, "I'm Synthea. Everyone calls me Syn."

Dad gives her hand a shake. "Syn. And how did you two meet?"

Head snapping toward Syn, I bite my lip. Am I really ready for this? To potentially blow up my family? Surely, Dad will side with Mom.

Before I can say anything, Mom comes outside, carrying a tray of food. Lips pursed, my sister-in-law, Jenn, follows behind with another tray.

"Penelope, you're finally here. Now we can eat." Annoyance brittles Mom's tone as she fills the middle of the outdoor dining table with various bowls and plates.

By the pool, Colin's kids snack before hopping back into the water.

While everyone shuffles around the table to their seats, Syn leans down, whispering in my ear. "You don't have to tell her tonight, sweetness. I'm okay being your friend if that's what you need."

I shake my head, meeting her gaze as I scoot my chair closer to the table. "I'm done hiding who I am."

Her eyes blaze, and she nods.

Besides the clink of silverware and dishes, silence envelopes the table as everyone fills their plates. The lack of conversation does nothing to settle my nerves. Taking the basket of rolls from Syn, a scrutinizing gaze from across the table prickles my skin.

"I hope you switched stylists after she gave you such a dreadful haircut, Penelope. If you need a recommendation, I'd be happy to make an appointment for you with Giselle."

Fork clattering to my plate, my mouth drops open, and my gaze snaps across the table to my mom. My eyes burn. *Don't cry. Don't cry. Don't cry.*

Utterly speechless, I can't even form a response, but I don't have to. Syn's hand clutches mine under the table. "I think she looks beautiful."

Jenn chimes in next. "Me, too." She smiles, tucking a chin length chestnut curl behind her ear. Mom has always hated that my brother's wife doesn't have long blonde hair. "It brings out your cheekbones and those adorable Martin dimples."

"Thank you." Cheeks scorching, my eyes lower to my plate.

Mom huffs and dabs the corners of her mouth with a napkin. "And I thought we agreed that you were bringing a date?" One penciled-on eyebrow arches expectantly.

I spare a glance at Syn. *You've got this*, she mouths before squeezing my hand.

Straightening my back, I hold my chin high and turn back toward Mom. "I did." I clear my throat, gathering Dad's and Colin's attention. Fingers laced through mine, I lay our joined hands on the table. "Syn is m-my girlfriend." Voice wobbling, I'm not sure how I get the words out without blacking out.

A hush falls over us, and I swear everyone can hear the rapid thumping of my heart. *Or is that just me?* Blood whooshes in my ears, while my fingers go numb. *Can you die from stress?*

"Girlfriend?" Mom scoffs. "You're not gay."

"Actually, I'm pansexual." I smirk at Syn, who smiles and squeezes my hand.

Mom's manic laugh pierces the air. "You're straight, Penelope. You always have been. You're going to settle down with a nice man and give me grandchildren. Like you're supposed to."

If I wasn't on the verge of having a panic attack, I would laugh at my mom trying to reason her way through the situation.

"No." I set my napkin on my plate, ready to make a quick exit. "Those are the things *you* want, Mom. You've been trying to mold me into something I'm not for as long as I can remember, and... and I'm done. I'm not doing it anymore."

She scoffs again, throwing her napkin onto the table. "Nonsense. This is just a phase."

"No, it's not!" Chest heaving, I stand, and Syn is right there next to me, hand braced on my lower back, letting me know she's there in case I need her. But I need to do this on my own. "This is who I am. Why can't you just love me?" Tears burn my eyes, but I refuse to let them fall.

Mom sucks in a sharp, pained gasp. "I have done *everything* to set you up for success, Penelope. If that's not love, then I don't know what is."

A cruel laugh bursts from me. "That's not love. It's control. Manipulation. *Abuse*." Like traitorous diamonds, the first tears spill over and roll down my cheeks.

She falls against the back of her chair like I've stabbed her through the heart. "Abuse? You ungrateful little—"

"Enough!" Dad shoots to his feet, his fists landing on the table and rattling the dishes. "Penelope is right."

By this point, Jenn has left the table and shooed the kids inside, away from the bickering adults. Colin's fists are balled on the table, like he's on the verge of snapping. Mom sucks in another gasp. "Charles," she pleads.

"No. I used work as a crutch to avoid what was happening right under my own roof." Blue eyes settle on me. "I'm sorry for that, Penny." His head swings to Mom, who cowers. "Leave our daughter alone, Caryn. Butt the fuck out and let her live the life she wants."

"I won't sit here and be disrespected like this!" Mom shrieks, her chair scraping across the cement as she stands.

"Then pack your bags. I think it'd be best if you spend the night somewhere else." Dad narrows his eyes on his wife.

Holy… Wow. Brain short circuiting, I collapse into my chair. He's fighting… for *me*?

Never did I think he'd kick her out. Siding with me is one thing, but demanding she leave their home is something different entirely.

Mom clutches the gaudy, bejeweled monstrosity around her neck. "You're kicking me out?!"

"Yes. It's something I should've done a long time ago. We've been broken for years, Caryn. Even you can admit that. Book a hotel or go to the apartment in the city. We'll talk in a few days when you've cooled off."

"Well, I never—"

"*Now*, Caryn." He points at the back door of the house.

Nose stuck in the air, Mom doesn't bother sparing us another glance as she leaves the table. It takes every ounce of strength I possess to hold in another wave of tears as she disappears into the house. A monumental weight lifts off my shoulders with each step she takes.

I should be sad that my family just imploded. But I'm... *not*. It was never my responsibility to keep my parents together.

As much as I was in denial about it, this day has been written in stone since my childhood. It was only a matter of time. I place a hand over my racing heart, blowing out a cleansing breath.

"Good riddance," Colin mumbles, crossing his arms over his chest.

"I truly am sorry. To both of you." Dad's gaze swings from me to Colin. "I thought staying with your mother was for the best. Clearly, I was wrong."

A ball of emotions has lodged itself in my throat, and all I can do is nod.

Dad's attention is back on me the next second. "Syn is good to you? She makes you happy?"

I nod again. "Yes, Dad. So happy."

His eyes move to my demon. "And Pen is good to you? Does my daughter make you happy?"

Syn smirks, eyes falling to me. "Yes, sir."

"Good. That's what matters." He plops into his seat and picks up his fork. "So, Syn, what do you do for work?"

Across the table, Colin chuckles and follows suit, taking a giant bite out of his dinner roll.

Syn's eyes widen as they meet mine. "Ummm..."

Chapter 25

Synthea

That was the weirdest fucking dinner I've ever experienced. After kicking Pen's mom out, it was business as usual for her dad. My hope is that Pen, Colin, and their dad can heal and become the family they should've been all along—minus that dreadful woman who hurt my mate.

"Well, sweetness, we survived," I say as I buckle the helmet under Penelope's chin.

"I can't believe he kicked her out." Grabbing the leather jacket off my bike, she shrugs it on.

"Yeah, that was... unexpected." I cup her chin, bringing her beautiful gaze to mine. "I'm so proud of you, Penelope. You didn't back down or let her belittle you. I'm in awe of your strength."

Her cheek warms under my palm. "Thank you." Slender fingers toy with the collar of my jacket before her eyes rise, timidness swirling within the cerulean. "But can you distract me, please? I don't want to think anymore."

"Say less. I know just the thing."

Stars twinkle above us, filling the dark sky with rare gemstones as we mount my bike and zip down the driveway.

Like a glowing beacon, the full moon guides me to an abandoned scenic pull-off on the side of the road. The bike rumbles beneath us as I come to a stop and pop the kickstand with a booted foot.

Not a soul around. Miles of smooth quartz sand. Gentle waves lapping at the shore. This is the perfect place for what I have in mind.

Swinging my leg over the bike, I dismount before helping Penelope do the same. Once our helmets are hanging from the handlebars, I slip off my jacket and toe off my boots.

"What are you doing?" Pen asks, humor in her voice. She mimics me until she's left in only her floral jumpsuit.

I grab her hand and tug her toward the water's edge. "You'll see."

Sand seeps between my toes, and a warm gust of wind ruffles my hair.

Once the gentle pulse of the ocean engulfs my feet, I smile and turn toward Penelope. Looking up at me, there's a freeness to her gaze that I haven't seen before. Like a weight has finally been lifted off her shoulders after coming out. A soft smile pulls at the corners of her mouth. It grows into something bigger, brighter, and her dimples grace me with their presence.

"You know... I've never been skinny dipping."

My eyebrows rise. "Never?" I've lost count of how many times I swam naked in the lakes of Hell during my rebellious teen years.

"It's unbecoming of a young lady to be out after dark. Let alone run around naked." She rolls her eyes and laughs. "But it always sounded like fun to me." She slips the thin straps of her jumpsuit off her shoulders. The gauzy material pools at her waist, revealing small breasts capped by rosy points.

I fumble for the buttons on my vest, undoing them as fast as possible and nearly ripping the lace bralette in my haste to get it off. "I think we both deserve a little fun, don't you?"

"We do. It's time to start coloring outside the lines, Princess." A wicked smirk stretches across her lips before she shoves her jumpsuit and panties to the ground. With a boisterous trail of laughter following her, she takes off into the water, leaving me behind as I wiggle out of my suit pants.

"Oh, you little..." The humid, end of summer air dampens my skin as I kick my clothes to the side and sprint after my mate.

A few yards from shore, Penelope splashes and laughs. My arms cut through the water, feet kicking as fast as they can to get to her.

I reach out, hoping to snag her waist, but I'm met by a face full of water and more laughter. Spitting the salty water from my mouth, I track the bob of her head as she swims away from me.

Never run from a demon, sweetness. We'll always find you.

Diving beneath the surface, my shadows unfurl from my body in thick tentacles, propelling me through the water as I hunt my prey.

Feet flutter in the distance. I smirk.

I circle behind her before breaking through the surface and wrapping my arms around her waist. Her shriek turns to a giggle as I nip the side of her neck. "Got you, little human."

Penelope spins in my arms. Fingers tangling in my soaked purple strands, she brings my mouth to hers. What starts as a sweet kiss quickly turns heated and primal. A fight for dominance that I know I'll win.

Her legs wrap around my hips, clenching and rocking her sweet cunt against me in her search for pleasure. My shadows tread the surrounding waves, keeping our heads above the surface as I get lost in my mate. Lips consume, tongues thrash, hands wander, groping greedily for flesh and connection.

"I want you forever, Penelope." Breaking our kiss, I pant the words. "Will you be my mate?"

Eagerly, she nods. "Yes. I choose to be selfish and unbelievably happy... I choose you, Syn." The smile that follows would knock me on my ass if I wasn't floating in the ocean.

"Unbelievably happy." I smooth her damp hair away from her forehead. "I like the sound of that, sweetness." Then my lips are on hers, unrelenting and hungry. My fingers sink into the flesh of her ass while my tail nestles against her clit, buzzing in time with the sloshing of the waves.

Penelope moans against my mouth, thighs gripping me with all their might as my shadows propel us to shore.

My knees collide with the sand, the surface rough and gritty against my skin as I crawl out of the water. Penelope clings to me like a baby koala, attacking my jaw, neck, chest... anything she can reach with her greedy lips.

After fifty years, I finally have everything that I could have dreamed of before I left Hell. Once she bears my mark, Penelope will be bound to me forever. Two souls woven together by unconditional love.

Oomph. My back hits the sand. Horny Penelope is surprisingly strong. Distracted by my thoughts, she got the better of me. She slips one leg under my thigh and grinds her cunt against mine. Arousal leaks from my core when she does it again and again, numbing my mind with pleasure.

Her small tits bounce in my face, glistening with droplets of water and begging to be sucked. Slinging an arm around her back, I sit up and wrap my lips around her puckered nipple. A gentle nip of my teeth has her hips rocking faster, hoarse moans creating a symphony against the backdrop of the crashing waves. "Yes, just like that," she cries, one hand clutching my horn.

I switch to the other side, working her toward her inevitable climax but, before long, Penelope shoves my shoulders, knocking me to my elbows. Legs scissoring mine, I lean back and enjoy the show.

Arms behind her, weight braced on her palms, Pen grinds down on me, sending a jolt of pleasure through my pierced clit. She pants, chest heaving as she does it again and again, cerulean eyes liquid with an inferno of lust.

"That's right, sweetness, use me. Take what you need."

Her head tips back, throat rippling with a deep moan. Fuck, she's so perfect like this, on the verge of being swept up by a river of ecstasy.

I'm close, too. Ready to tip over the edge as my orgasm prickles every hair on my body until they rise. My cunt spasms, tightening as my arms give out, and I collapse on the damp sand. With a cry, my back arches as I find my peak, Penelope tumbling right alongside me.

"We're not done, sweetness," I say, breaths sawing in and out of my lungs. "I still need to mate you." Raising my head, I find a blissed-out smile on her face, matched by hazy eyes.

Penelope leans forward, palms braced on my chest as she peers down at me. "Is it always going to be this amazing?"

I sit up, encircling her with my arms and shadows. "I sure fucking hope so."

She smiles. "Me, too."

Guiding her hips in a gentle back and forth, I slip a shadow inside her pussy. She moans, eyelids fluttering.

The dark appendage bends and twists, the other end sliding into my cunt with ease, connecting me to my mate. I settle my palm over her heart, the steady beat a comfort. Stars twinkle in her eyes as I ask, "Are you ready to be mine, sweetness?"

"As long as you'll be mine, too," she answers, settling her hand over my heart. Instinct must be pulling her through the steps of the mating bond without her even knowing it.

My tail slips between us with ease as the shadows begin to secrete their special fluids. A warm tingle blooms in my core. "Always and forever."

Hands on each other's hearts, we rock together until we're at the cliff's edge, ready to dive headfirst into the abyss. This is it. Eyes locked with Penelope's, my palm heats, purple illuminating the silhouette of my hand.

She hisses, but her inner walls grip my shadow until it can no longer move. I fall with her. The sharp sting when the mate mark takes hold is the final push I need.

"Did it work?" Penelope removes her hand to reveal a glowing purple handprint. *Her* handprint. Etched into my skin forever.

"See for yourself." I slide my hand away as she leans back to examine her chest. Mirroring mine, there's a pulsing handprint on her chest, too. It flickers in time with the beating muscle inside me and will continue to do so until I take my last breath. "I don't want to live in a world where you're not, Penelope. When your heart stops beating, so does mine." I tap the luminous mark on her chest.

"You gave up your immortality for me?" Tears glisten in her eyes.

"It wasn't even a question, sweetness. I spent fifty years waiting for you. And now that I have you, I don't want to exist without you."

Forehead dropping to mine, she whispers, "I love you, Syn."

"I love you, sweetness."

Chapter 26

A wide smile stretches across my face, sunlight casting an orange glow onto my closed lids. The steady thumping of the mark on my chest has me biting my cheek to hold back a squeal.

Last night actually happened.

Syn is really my mate.

A rush of warmth fills me as I roll onto my side, finally allowing my eyes to open and take in my mate.

My mate.

After spending the last few years watching friends find their eternal partners, the term mate feels right. The same way her disheveled purple hair and soft snores are a balm to my soul.

Lying on her stomach, her back rises and falls with the steady rhythm of her breaths, a pillow clutched tight in one arm. Without her there yesterday, I don't think I would have had the courage to come out to my mom.

Ugh. My mom. I should probably get up and deal with whatever fallout is waiting for me. After leaving my parents' house, I turned off my phone, shoved it in the bottom of my purse, and haven't touched it since. There are probably a million and one messages from her.

Penelope, that's no way to talk to the woman who birthed you and raised you.

Penelope, you owe me an apology for yesterday's outburst.

Penelope. Penelope. Penelope.

Right now, I'd much rather be Syn's sweetness than Penelope. Maybe I'll ditch my phone and get a new number, keep the outside world shut out for a little while longer.

Unfortunately, I can't.

My stomach chooses that moment to unleash a loud rumble. Apparently, I need to eat, too. Three rounds of intense sex will work up a girl's appetite.

Syn's skin is warm against my lips when I press them to her forehead. I inhale, filling my lungs with her distinct scent. Hopefully, the tart cherries and rich bourbon will give me the courage to call my dad. There's no way I'm dealing with Mom today.

Five to seven business day waiting period for her, for sure.

Sliding out from under the covers, I miss the coziness immediately, but slide on a pair of sweats and a tank top before the urge to dive back into bed with my mate becomes overwhelming.

After solidifying our bond on the beach, we couldn't keep our hands off each other, so Syn teleported us back to the apartment. She said a demon mate bond can create a sort of breeding frenzy when done between two demons. I guess with me being human and her only being half demon, the frenzy wasn't as strong, but we still managed another round in the shower before passing out in bed.

I wander to the open living area. To my left, Fen is sprawled out in his favorite spot on the couch, fast asleep. Raven fur glistens under thick beams of morning sun. With a silent chuckle, I sneak past him into the kitchen.

Quiet as can be, I get out eggs, bacon, and a pan.

The smell will wake him in no time, so I'm not sure why I'm bothering to be quiet.

Before I can get the food cooking, a yawn tears through me. Coffee first, then food.

As much as the sex last night was the distraction I needed, it's time to put on my big girl panties and deal with the aftermath. Did Dad kick Mom out for good? Does this mean they're getting divorced?

Guilt eats away at me as I turn on the coffeemaker. "It's not your fault, Pen," I whisper to myself.

Based on Dad's reaction, it seems like he and Mom had issues before yesterday. Maybe that's why he was always working when I was younger.

Do I blame him for not intervening and protecting me from Mom?

I don't know.

But I do know that I'm not ready to lose both parents. Cutting Mom out is probably for the best, but I can't lose Dad, too.

He wasn't present during my childhood like he should have been, but he's not a monster like Mom.

It's going to take some time before I can forgive him for never stopping her abuse.

The hiss of the coffeemaker pulls me back to the present. Aromatic, black liquid fills the mug that I don't remember putting under the dispenser. *Good thing I can make coffee with my eyes closed.*

I grab the vanilla creamer from the fridge and add a splash to my steaming mug. The first sip has all my worries melting away.

"Good morning, cupcake." The gruff voice in my head has me spinning on my heels. My mug slips from my fin-

gers, crashing to the ground and shattering into a mess of ceramic and dark liquid.

Next to the island sits Fenrir, tail thumping against the floor and tongue spilling from behind sharp teeth.

Once my heart decides to stay in my chest, I ask, "Did you just...?"

His ruby eyes widen. "*You can hear me?*"

I step forward, hissing when a sharp pain slices the bottom of my foot, but I don't stop, too in awe that I can finally communicate with Fen the way Syn does. Dropping to my knees in front of him, I cup his fuzzy jaw. "Say something else—"

In the process of stuffing her arm into the sleeve of her shirt, Syn barrels into the kitchen on socked feet. "What happened? I heard something shatter." Frantic energy surrounds her as her eyes drop to the mess behind me.

"Oh, umm..." I peek over my shoulder at the bottom of my foot. Sure enough, blood bubbles from a deep gash.

"Sweetness, you're hurt." She extends a hand to me, not giving me much of a choice as she pulls me to stand on my uninjured foot before boosting me onto the counter.

"It's just a scratch," I object when she sidesteps the broken mug and wets a bundle of paper towels in the sink. I bite my lip to hold in the whimper as she presses the damp compress to the bottom of my foot, applying pressure to stop the bleeding. "I can hear Fen," I blurt as she pulls the bloodied material away.

Her gaze flits between me and the hellhound. "Huh. Well, that's a fun little side effect." A long finger skims over the cut. Purple illuminates the bottom of my foot before dissipating and leaving smooth, healed skin in its wake. "Fen, I guess you'll have someone else to annoy now."

Jaw snapping shut, Fen's ears twitch. *"I am not annoying."*

"No, you're not, Fen." He's so tall that I can scratch the top of his head from my perch on the counter. My eyes fall to Syn. "So is this because of the mate bond."

"That's my guess. I've heard of telepathy between familiar and mate happening when two demons solidify their bond, but I wasn't sure if it would happen since you're human."

"Yes," Fen answers in my head, *"I live to serve you, cupcake."*

"Cupcake?" I raise an eyebrow.

Syn's dark eyes roll as she chuckles. "That's what he calls you."

"Well, isn't that cute," I coo, tickling Fen's chin.

"Yeah, he's got a thing for sweets." She steps between my thighs, fingers circling my throat and bringing my mouth to hers. The words ghost over my lips when she says, "Seems like he and I have that in common." Then her lips are on mine in a hungry kiss.

A pang of hunger in my stomach has me cutting the exchange short. "I was about to make breakfast. Want to help?"

She guides me off the countertop. "Always."

"So what happens now?" I pass her the eggs, and she cracks them into the pan.

"Whatever we want, Pen. But we should probably start by getting my bike. We left it parked on the side of the highway an hour from here."

I bump her hip with mine and smile. "Wouldn't mind a scenic drive down the coast... after breakfast. But, ummm..."

"What?"

My hands tangle in the hem of my tank top, the pit in my stomach returning. "I-I think I want to start therapy to work through all the trauma from my mom."

Somehow knowing exactly what I need to stop me from spinning out with anxiety, Syn turns away from the stove and pulls me in for a hug. "I think that sounds like a great idea, Pen."

I nod, lips resting against her throat. "I'm going to ask Dad and Colin to go, too. We have a lot to work through, but..."

"But you'll come out stronger on the other side, sweetness." Her arms slip to my waist, and I lean back to meet her eyes. They twinkle with a depthless love. *Unconditional* love. "And when it gets hard, and you think you might fall, I'll be there to catch you."

"Thank you for being my compass and helping me find my path, Syn."

She shrugs. “That was all you, Pen. I just gave you a little shove in the right direction.” Her face lights up with a smile, and she winks.

For the first time, it truly feels like my life *is* heading in the right direction. All thanks to a disastrous blind date and a purple-haired demon bartender.

Epilogue

Synthea

A few months later

The pixie female slides some crumpled bills across the bar to me, amethyst eyes twinkling with mischief. "Can you send a Sex on the Beach to the handsome orc in the corner?"

My gaze follows hers to the other end of the bar, where a large orc male occupies the last stool. He must be nearly two feet taller than her, and I've always been curious how they make the size difference work.

But it's none of my business.

The orc's eyes heat, following his wife's movements as she props her arms on the bar, a tasteful amount of cleavage on display above the neckline of her sequined top.

I chuckle, grabbing a glass and getting to work on the fruity drink. "Role playing again, Maria?"

Glossy pink lips pull into a smirk. Glittering wings flutter behind her back, throwing a burst of rainbows onto the walls of the Taproom. "Gotta keep things fresh after a decade of marriage and two kids." She winks, eyes tracking me as I walk to the other side of the bar and slide the drink in front of her husband.

Thick green fingers wrap around the chilled glass before toying with the little umbrella skewering a cherry.

"From the kind lady over there." I point to Maria, who dips her fingers in a flirty wave. "Storage closet down the hall is open, but don't leave a mess like last time," I joke, pointing a finger at Phil. There's no heat behind my reprimand, since they cleaned up and replaced the broken shelving unit.

I still like to give him shit, though.

A booming laugh fills the air as he gives me a two-finger salute. "You got it, Syn." Grabbing the drink, he leaves his stool in pursuit of his wife.

I shake my head as he whispers something in her ear. Maria giggles before leaving the bar and following her husband down the darkened hallway.

Ten years of marriage, and they still can't keep their hands off each other. I can only hope my relationship with Penelope stands the test of time. It's been a few months, and the fire is raging as hot as our first time. Maybe even hotter.

Knowing she's waiting upstairs for me. Helping her run through her sales pitches. Watching cheesy movies and eating takeout on my nights off. And, of course, Sundays at the farmers' market. I still leave little notes by her coffee every morning.

Yeah, I'm head over fucking heels for my mate, and domestic bliss is better than I could have imagined.

My phone buzzes in my pocket. A message from my sweetness fills the screen when I pull it out.

Sweetness: What time will you be home? I miss you.

I chuckle. Seems someone else is just as desperate as I am.

"'Bout time for you to leave, boss." Thick arms filled with liquor bottles, Frank slips behind the bar.

Once he's safely placed them all on the shelf, I slap his back. "First night as manager. Call me if you run into any issues."

He tips his head to Xavier, who's taken up residence on the stool Phil vacated a few minutes ago. "We've got it covered, don't we, Xav?"

The wolven nods, arms crossed over his barrel chest. "See ya tomorrow, boss."

"'Night, boys. And, ah, maybe avoid the storage closet for an hour or so." A final wave before I head to my office to grab my bag. I make sure to give the storage closet a wide berth as I slip out the back exit and down the alley.

As much as I want to go home to my mate, I have to make one more stop first.

Crossing the street, I follow the neon glow of the sign until I come to the front door of the Inked Pixie. The bell overhead tinkles as I step inside. Approaching the empty reception desk, I shout, "Hello?"

Crickets.

Usually, the shop isn't busy on Tuesdays, especially not this close to closing time.

Tucking my hands into my pockets, I round the ivy-covered brick wall behind the desk. Boots filled with lead, I stop in my tracks when I find my sister mauling Rafe.

And not mauling, like, trying to kill him.

No. Her hands are in his hair and running over his wings. He moans as her teeth sink into his bottom lip, a trickle of red spilling around them.

Holy fuck! I rub my eyes, but they're still there. Going at it like two horny teenagers. Lucie has him backed against one of the tables, his hands wound around her hips.

"Ahem." I clear my throat.

You'd think Rafe was on fire with how fast my sister puts distance between them. "Syn. W-What are you doing here?" Voice pitching up an octave, the gray skin of Lucie's cheeks turns a dark mauve.

I chuckle and rock onto my toes. "Just came to see how things are going."

"Everything's fine." This time, her voice cracks.

"Mhmmm." I smirk.

Lucie scoffs, crossing her arms over her chest. "It's nothing."

Rafe's lips curl into a downright devilish grin. "That's not what you were saying last night, Cruella."

Lucie slaps a hand over his mouth before flashing me a tight-lipped smile. "Just ignore him... *Please.*"

I throw my hands up in surrender. "None of my business. Lock up before you leave. And, Luce, don't kill him."

Their bickering fills the air before I burst into flames.

A subtle vanilla scent surrounds me when I materialize inside the front door of my apartment. Except for a single lamp in the living room, it's dark, long shadows dancing across the ceiling as the tree branches sway outside.

The couch is noticeably empty. That seems to be the norm since Penelope and I solidified our bond and she moved into my room... officially. Fenrir has claimed Penelope's old bedroom for himself.

I'm not sure why he didn't do that a long time ago, but I guess I should be grateful.

If that bedroom hadn't been empty, I never would've offered it to Pen. She never would've moved in, and I don't know if we'd be mates.

Sure, I would've pursued her, but maybe she would've come to her senses and told me to fuck off.

Thank fuck, she didn't.

I can't imagine my life without her.

I drop my bag on the kitchen table before continuing down the dark hallway toward our bedroom. A rim of light illuminates the partially closed door at the end of the hall, beckoning me to the sweet little human waiting on the other side.

With a gentle press of my fingers, the door creeps inward, revealing my sweetness. Lit by the warm glow of the bedside lamps, her petite frame is swathed in a navy-blue silk robe. Hands gripping something in front of her body, her feet lead her on a path back and forth in front of the window.

She paces one way. "What if she says no?" She paces back. "What if she doesn't like it?" She paces away again. "This was a terrible idea."

Biting my bottom lip, I brace my back against the doorframe. "Whatcha doin', sweetness?"

Penelope sucks in a sharp breath, fumbling as she hastily tucks her hands—and the mysterious object—behind her back. "N-Nothing."

"Mhmmm." I push off the doorframe, the demonic part of me coming to the surface as I stalk across the room. "I was going to tell you how I walked in on my sister kissing Rafe, but I'm more curious about what you're hiding." With a single finger, I guide her chin up until our eyes lock. "Care to share with the class?"

Her brow scrunches. "Lucie and Rafe?"

"Yup." I pop the *p*. "But that's not important right now." My fingers slide along her jaw and down her throat until they rest over the galloping hoofbeats below her skin. "What's got you so nervous?"

Behind my back, the silicone slips between my trembling fingers.

Just tell her.

She's your mate. She won't judge you for wanting this. She never has before.

Tell her.

I release a sigh before meeting Syn's dark gaze. The lust coursing through me is mirrored in the midnight of her irises, her pupils already expanded to full capacity. "I-I want to fuck you." My voice betrays me, wobbling the slightest, but I push the words out.

Syn smirks. "You fucked me this morning. Remember when I filled all your pretty holes with my shadows and you rode me like a good girl?"

Cheeks heating, I shiver at the imagery she paints while her fingers bracket my throat.

I push her hand away and huff. "Not like that." *Now or never, Pen. Show her.* "With *this.*" Bringing my other hand in front of me, I present the dildo to her. Both ends are long and thick, one sliding inside me while I use the other on my mate.

One eyebrow raised, Syn eyes the black silicone gripped in my hands.

Her silence has my gut clenching and my head dropping until the wood floor fills my vision. "You hate it… Don't you?" My voice falls to a whisper.

Gentle fingers slide under my chin, guiding it up again. For the first time ever, Syn's smile is shy. "No. It's just… no one has ever used one on me before."

The nerves in her voice have me backtracking. "We don't have to. Forget I asked."

"Shush, sweetness. Do you know how proud I am right now?"

Proud? I shake my head.

"You're asking for what you want. I know it took a lot of courage, and I'm proud of you."

The praise has me smiling, my stupid cheeks blushing again. "Thank you."

A wry smile replaces the look of unease on Syn's face. "And I would love it if you fucked me." The wink she sends my way as she strips off her clothes has my confidence growing.

Wetness pools between my thighs once every inch of tattooed gray skin is on display. My blood simmers as the glowing hand mark between her breasts pulses in time with the thrum of my heart.

Untying the sash around my waist, I let the silken fabric slip to the floor, leaving me in only a black harness. The matching mark on my chest illuminates. Seeing the physical evidence of our bond never gets old.

"Mmm. Look at you." Syn gathers me in her arms, lips descending onto mine for a slow, drugging kiss.

Kissing my mate has to be one of my favorite things. Her tongue curls to perfection as it strokes around mine. Sharp teeth nip lightly at my lips. Besides sex, I feel closest to Syn in moments like this.

Turning down the heat, I break the kiss and hold up the double-ended toy. "Will you help me put this on?"

Syn nods toward the bed. "Lie down."

Not wasting a second, my back hits the mattress, and I hand the toy to her.

Hovering over me, she leaves a wet, hot trail of lips and tongue down my body. Back arching, I moan as her teeth nip the harness strap around my hips. She grips my thighs before pushing them up and out until my core is exposed.

I'm wet already. Glistening and ready. I have been for hours.

Syn wraps her lips around my clit and sucks, the burst of pleasure has more arousal leaking from me. Her tongue drags through my folds, but my juices flow faster than she can lap them up.

I prop myself onto my elbows, peering over my heaving breasts and tummy to the purple-haired demon feasting between my legs. Eyes shut, Syn moans as she drives her tongue deep inside me.

When she takes her mouth away, I whimper. "Just had to make sure you were nice and wet, sweetness," she says, bringing the toy to my core and running it through my pussy lips until it's sufficiently lubricated and slippery. With a flip of her wrist, Syn nestles the tapered tip against my opening. Her eyes swing up to mine. "Ready?"

All I can do is nod. Anticipation has been coursing through my veins since this afternoon when I picked up my order at the adult shop around the corner.

She presses forward, the toy slipping inside with ease. I sigh at the slight stretch, the relief of being filled... *finally*.

After maneuvering the other side into the front of the harness, Syn pulls me into a sitting position. "Now it's your turn. Where do you want me?"

Ummm. Where *do* I want her? I haven't really thought that far ahead. Do I want to take her from behind, watch her ass bounce off my pelvis?

As appealing and arousing as that image is. I need the emotional connection that we've spent months building. I need to look into her eyes while I slip inside her.

"On your back... please."

Syn chuckles, but lies in the middle of the bed. "So polite."

Prowling over her body, I settle on my knees between her spread thighs. Magnetized by our bond, my hands seek her skin, rubbing up the outsides of her legs before gripping her hips. My fingers dent the flesh as anticipation thrums in my veins.

Leaning down, I suck one nipple into my mouth, marveling at the cold sting of the barbell against my tongue. Syn's back arches with a moan, and she clutches my hair.

I switch to the other peaked bud, giving it ample attention before working my way down her luscious body. Saliva trails behind as my tongue drags through her navel.

Finally, I make it to her core, where the gemstone decorating her clit calls to my tongue. I lick and suck the little bundle of nerves until Syn's hips are writhing against my face and her fingers tighten in my hair.

Her shadows roll across the sheets, curling and uncurling like an octopus trolling along the ocean floor.

She's right on the edge.

But I want her to come when I'm inside her. Not a second sooner.

Frenetic energy rushes through me as I rip my mouth from her core, grab the lube from the nightstand, and coat the appendage protruding from my pelvis. Gripping the girthy base in my hand, I scoot closer to my mate and line the tip up to her glistening opening. "You're sure about this?"

"Fuck me, sweetness. I'm begging you."

My skin prickles. I think I like Syn begging for me.

Shaking the thought away, I press my hips forward, eyes locked on where her opening stretches to accommodate the girthy toy. Holy moly! Why is that so sexy?

My inner muscles clamp around the length inside me as I thrust forward. Syn moans, legs squeezing me when I bottom out. "Hold on," I say, bracing my weight on one hand. The other hand fumbles for the remote on the nightstand. A few presses of the button later, and both ends of the toy whir to life.

Eyes rolling to the back of my head, I catch my breath for a second.

Sharp nails dig into my hips. "Fuck, that feels good, but you gotta move, baby girl."

Slowly, I withdraw until only the bulbous tip remains inside my mate, then I roll my hips forward, impaling her on my length. Syn's eyes slam shut, head cushioned on the pillow when she lets out a pleasured cry.

I do the same thing again. And again. And again. Falling into a rhythm that has us both moaning in ecstasy. Sweat dampens my brow, and my fingers dig into her hips, the vibrations from the toy pushing me closer and closer to my peak.

"Be a good girl and come for me, mate," I demand, unsure of where the words come from. In a suffocating grip, Syn's thighs pin my hips and her muscles go rigid. A final cry leaves her throat, and I lose the fight, falling into oblivion with her.

Arms giving out, I collapse forward, but Syn is there to catch me, like always. She bundles me against her sweat-slicked body, lips slamming onto mine. I moan against her mouth, the aftershocks of my orgasm rippling through me.

"Damn, sweetness. I think we need to do this more often."

My laughter is muffled against her supple lips. "That can be arranged." Fingers searching the sheets, I find the remote and click off the vibrations.

Syn wraps an arm around me, tugging me against her warm body as we snuggle into bed for the night. "How did therapy go today?"

After my family imploded on Labor Day, Colin, Dad, and I started going to family therapy every other week to work through the lingering guilt and animosity. I cut all contact with Mom, which hurt initially, but I've worked through that pain and trauma with my therapist.

I still have a long way to go, but I'm proud of the progress I've made in only a few months.

"It was actually really good. Lots of tears, but... good. I don't think I've ever seen Dad cry in my entire life, but

I think Colin finally forgives him for not protecting me from Mom."

"And what about you? Do you forgive him?"

I shrug, pulling my bottom lip under my teeth. "I'll get there in time. I'm not angry anymore, just... sad. Sad I missed out on a normal life because Dad shoved his head in the sand and Mom couldn't be the mom she should have been."

"You deserve time to heal, Pen. And I'm glad you're facing those hard feelings with Colin and your dad. Hopefully, you'll come out of this situation with the relationship you were always meant to have."

"I hope so."

Quiet blankets the room as Syn's fingers stroke through my hair.

"In a weird way—and as much as I hate to admit it—she's kind of responsible for us meeting."

"Your mom?"

I nod. "Yeah. If I hadn't gone on that dreadful date, you wouldn't have stepped in to protect me, and I wouldn't have fallen madly in love with you."

"I would've found you eventually, sweetness. The last thing I'm doin' is giving credit to that bitch. Has she contacted you at all?"

I shake my head. "No. Dad took out a restraining order against her after the divorce. She's disappeared into some hole with half his money."

"Good riddance. Toxic bitch."

"Sayonara, cunt." I wave my hand like I'm shooing an annoying fly.

Syn laughs. "I don't think I've ever heard you say that word before. I really am rubbing off on you."

I giggle and snuggle into her side. "I love you, Syn."

"Love you, too, sweetness."

There's a whine and the scratch of claws on the partially closed bedroom door. "*What about me? Don't you love me?*"

Luminous red puppy eyes peer over the side of the bed, and I burst into a fit of giggles.

"Get in here, ya big lug."

Tongue hanging out the side of his mouth, Fen doesn't waste a second jumping onto the bed and nestling his way between me and Syn. I bury my fingers into the fur on his neck. "I love you, too, Fen."

With a sigh, his eyes flutter closed. "*Mmm. I love my cupcake... and you too, Princess.*"

Syn laughs, patting him on the head. "Wow, thanks, Fen."

My heart and soul are so full that tears spring to my eyes. We may not be a conventional family, but we take care of each other and make each other unbelievably happy.

And I wouldn't change a thing.

Are you ready to finally find out how Phil and Maria met? The Orc in the Diner, the final installment of the Monstrous New York series, is coming soon.

E.M. Sauber was born and raised in the Midwest. Reading has always been a part of her life. A way to escape when the real world gets to be too much.

She currently lives in Minnesota with her wonderful husband, two children, and two dogs.

When she isn't writing steamy shifter stories, you can find her cuddled on the couch under a fuzzy blanket with her kindle or daydreaming about a new idea for a book.

www.ingramcontent.com/pod-product-compliance
Lightning Source LLC
LaVergne TN
LVHW020705110826
845149LV00012B/2107

* 9 7 9 8 9 9 9 6 4 2 8 3 7 *